BEFORE.
DURING.
AFTER.

PHILIP CHARTER

Pelekinesis

Before. During. After. by Philip Charter
978-1-949790-86-3   Paperback
978-1-949790-87-0   Ebook

Copyright © 2024 Philip Charter. All rights reserved.
Cover design: Philip Charter
Layout and book design by Mark Givens
First Pelekinesis Printing 2024

For information:
Pelekinesis
112 Harvard Ave #65
Claremont, CA 91711 USA

Library of Congress Cataloging-in-Publication Data

Names: Charter, Philip, 1985- author.
Title: Before. during. after. / Philip Charter.
Description: Claremont, CA : Pelekinesis, 2024. | Summary: "'Before.
   During. After.' is a novella-in-flash which presents a sequence of
   life-changing moments for a cast of twenty interconnected characters.
   The book is set in an unnamed small town in the USA, and focuses on the
   lives of students, teachers and parents of the local high school"--
   Provided by publisher.
Identifiers: LCCN 2023038918 (print) | LCCN 2023038919 (ebook) | ISBN
   9781949790863 (paperback) | ISBN 9781949790870 (ebook)
Subjects: LCGFT: Novellas.
Classification: LCC PR6103.H3867 B44 2024 (print) | LCC PR6103.H3867
   (ebook) | DDC 823/.92--dc23/eng/20231124
LC record available at https://lccn.loc.gov/2023038918
LC ebook record available at https://lccn.loc.gov/2023038919

www.pelekinesis.com

BEFORE. DURING. AFTER.

PHILIP CHARTER

CAST OF CHARACTERS

Coach Primley
Age: 58
Occupation: High school coach

Kyle Radley
Age: 17
Occupation: Student

Roger Radley
Age: 55
Occupation: Fund Manager

Catherine Schwarz
Age: 34
Occupation: Attorney

Beth Schwarz
Age: 64
Occupation: Retired

Manuel Hernández
Age: 24
Occupation: Carer

Eduardo Lopez
Age: 47
Occupation: Janitor

Ruby Carson
Age: 9
Occupation: Student

Kayleigh Harris
Age: 32
Occupation: Child Protective Services Agent

Henry Caudry
Age: 52
Occupation: Child Protective Services Manager

Molly Caudry
Age: 26
Occupation: Back-end developer

Janine Bowen
Age: 29
Occupation: Call Center Agent

Enid Stanford
Age: 70
Occupation: Retired

Joey Brown
Age: 40
Occupation: Security Guard

Leticia Brown
Age: 40
Occupation: Homemaker

Amanda O'Rourke
Age: 27
Occupation: Police Officer

Nadia Belhadj
Age: 22
Occupation: College Student

Harry Katar
Age: 35
Occupation: Debt Collector

Ray Greene
Age: 17
Occupation: Server

Principal Joyce
Age: 50
Occupation: High school Principal

BEFORE

COACH PRIMLEY

These kids are about to pass into a world outside the womb. Even if they stay cooped up in this town, they'll filter through community college on the way to a soulless job, via Dairy Queen and family trauma avenue. For the players on my varsity team, high school might be the highest high they ever taste. When I was their age, I didn't care about anything but game day and the Sunday meal after church. How can I change the course of their lives with one little speech?

They sit there and look at me from the gymnasium stands. I've smelled the same floor varnish my whole thirty years here. Perhaps I should just tell them the ultimate secret to gaining respect — being right and saying the same thing every year.

There will be other kids, but after this, I'll be a ghost — no more than a faded photo and an empty trophy cabinet. When my speech gets going, those thirty years will be the ones talking, not me. I make out like it's off the cuff, but I rehearsed more times than I shot the ball through the hoop. *What is a man with no job, no kids, no wife?* That's actually the first line on the paper in my pocket.

I stand behind the principal. I'm so close I can smell the bullshit as he thanks the staff members one by one. We get that every year instead of a pay rise. His voice drones on like some bad actor in a teen movie. If he was on my team, I'd run the lies out of him.

There's an alchemy to being liked. You've got to give

up caring. Act aloof, but always be listening. You have to be one of them, even though when you were their age, the Internet didn't exist. You have to remember you were the same and forget the teammates who are broke, crippled, or dead. You have to forgive yourself for ruining a college coaching career because you gave up two of your players for doping. That's in the speech too. My mouth goes dry, just like it did at Marta's funeral. The school board forced me back after less than a month even though I could barely see the next minute in front of me.

I clear my throat and it echoes around the gym. Ten seconds to game time.

When I think about it, life is kind of like a game clock, with a couple of time-outs and just a few seconds to celebrate. Sometimes you foul out even when it ain't your fault.

I breathe in the court one last time and catch the scent of game day against our rivals, the Timberwolves. Those days I wake up and drive through the woodland roads for an hour to calm my mind.

Then Principal Joyce says, "Give a hand to *your* coach Primley," like I'll always belong to these kids.

The whooping and shouting starts. Time to show them the gold extracted from thirty years of lessons. Make this one count, Primley. Then be a ghost.

KYLE RADLEY

Coach is a better father to me than my old man was. Primley drives me home after practice. Primley knows when to talk. This might be the last time I ever get to listen to his 'Gatorade wisdom'.

Mom said the penitentiary called last week. Roger was in the infirmary after an argument in the yard. Not to worry, they said. I told her I wasn't worried, and we got into an argument.

I'll be out of this town before Roger gets out. Sucks for Mom.

Hayley's eyes meet mine. Same row, five seats down. She motions with her head. *Bathroom.*

I try a shrug, but she jerks her head harder. It must be serious if she's walking out during Primley's big moment. Couldn't we have talked during the academic speeches or the marching band? It was a one-time thing, but the look she gives me closes down the whole gym — no squeak of shoes on the floor, no traffic sounds through the high windows, no surgical lights, no noise from the bleachers.

What am I going to tell her? Does she know about Jayden and me? On the team, Primley writes the tactics, and I just follow. No overthinking. All you have to do is run till you're sick and hit the weights every day. How come nothing else in life works that way?

Waiting for her to slip past O'Donahue at the door takes an age, but only half a minute passes on the clock. Imagine what five years feels like.

After she's gone, I stand up and follow her to the bathrooms.

Roger Radley

When you get your ribs broken, the pain spreads fast. Every movement sends those little agony sergeants all over, up your back, into the base of your skull. But a man won't let you take the only wealth he has left. He'll die for it.

They tell me my lawyer's waiting. After that, it's back to the cell. Two nights in the infirmary bed and one painkiller a day. You can't fight back on one painkiller a day.

Despite the silence on previous visiting days, I thought my son might call this time. How would that conversation go? "Kyle, your pop can't talk today. He nearly got killed." Maybe he thinks I'll hand over the keys to the crypto ledgers to the state for a reduced sentence. Maybe he thinks basketball and girls are more important than building a legacy.

The nurse helps me off the bed and signs me out.

"Don't you send anybody else back here in return, now."

"Hey," I say, "I'm a fraudster, not a mobster."

She smiles but doesn't laugh. Maybe she doesn't want to make me laugh 'cause of the pain.

Robertson collects me and marches me down to see the lawyer in the visiting room. If they send the youngest, weakest c/o, they're calling you weak too. They tell you to 'keep your head down', but it's impossible when you're floating in a sea of trouble. Robertson's heels tap-tap-tap all the way down the gray corridor. Each step hammers the dread.

Catherine Schwarz is running my case. She's a local type, went to a good college like me, and opened a business like me. We're both not supposed to be here. Her last letter said she wasn't hopeful of getting an appeal date. God knows how long ago that was. The weeks blend together here (until somebody introduces a pipe to your ribs to try and change your mind about the passwords, then time goes even slower).

We reach the door, and I peer through the reinforced window pane. She's at the table, head stooped, studying the piece of paper that probably contains four more years on it. I've done the math so many times. $1 million per year, maybe more. It has to be worth it.

Roberts stuffs the key in the lock and opens the door. "Ten minutes," he says.

I doubt it will take her more than sixty seconds to crush any hope I have left.

Catherine Schwarz

When he gets home, we'll talk it out. It'll be better this time. I'll tell him about my afternoon meeting with the white-collar felon. He loves hearing other people's bad news. We'll sit on the couch, not in different rooms eating TV dinners, like last anniversary, or staring straight ahead, unable to meet each other's eyes while a doctor explains what happened with the baby. That was the night our relationship died.

It's eight pm. One drink after work is the usual. He's letting off steam is all. That's the car now. Low-profile tires crush the driveway gravel.

When he gets in, I won't ask about his day. I'll pretend the odors of Jack's Grill don't offend me. Catfish and scorched steak.

When he comes in the door, I'll open a bottle. That will brighten the mood. I'll have a game running on the TV. It doesn't matter which one. Mind-numbing statistics and the satisfying smack of bat on ball.

When he sits down, glass in front of him, plus a big bowl of peanuts, I'll tell him what happened in my client meeting at the prison.

When there's a break in the action, he'll tell me about some lunatic at the bar getting into a skirmish with the police. "I gave him your number for the future," he'll say. Perhaps we'll make vague plans for the weekend which might be canceled due to work commitments.

We won't talk about the time I nearly represented myself. After the shouting and open palms to the face, the fists to the ribs, and the apologies after. He was stressed.

There will be no calls to my mother.

We'll eat *spaghetti all'aglio*. We'll make love. We'll make another baby. This one will take.

His key rattles the lock.

I look up and prepare my kindest smile.

Beth Schwarz

My daughter said not to call. But I should call. I mean, when was the last time we didn't speak of an evening?

She said that tonight was the night she'd work it out with Peter, but they won't work it out because the whole thing went rotten after they lost the baby. It's strange. The opposite happened with her father. He upped and left before he knew I was pregnant. I never did tell him.

Manuel asks if I need my diaper changed. The only clue is the smell, and he doesn't like to hover around the wheelchair, sniffing to see if he needs to take me to the bathroom. That's out of his job description.

"I'm going to call Catherine," I say.

"Is that really a good idea, Mrs. Schwarz?" he asks, using his customer service voice.

When I ask for the phone, he starts to argue, telling me I agreed not to call because she has this important talk with her husband.

I tell him I remember how those end — with a man soothing his knuckles in a motel ice bucket before dropping the cubes stained with blood and hair into a tumbler. He brings me the phone after that.

Despite her problems, she'll choke back the tears. I can barely choke down my food these days. Catherine still has her health. Anyway, that's what she'll say to the others at my funeral.

I dial the number and it rings. It rings. If he's not home, she'll pick up. We'll plan how she can get out of this thing.

Manuel lights the stove and prepares the herbal tea. For my joints he says. He'll be out of work when I go. Maybe Catherine can find him something.

The fire roars under the teapot and the ringtone sounds again and again. I've told her countless times that to get what you want, to get what you deserve, one has to be persistent.

Manuel Hernández

I lost count how many times I've wheeled her into the doctor's office and waited outside. Mrs. Schwarz is a real blessing. She recently gave me a third option in life. The other two were to wash dishes or return to Guatemala. She jokes with me, like when she called it the American Trap instead of the American Dream. I told my sister on the phone, but she just asked why I can't send extra this month to cover Mamá's pills.

Instead of listening to music, I should be handing out my number, looking for another blessing, a new client who needs care. The last tests found cancer and these ones tell us when Mrs. Schwarz will pass away.

Mrs. Schwarz never talks about death. Americans can be strange like that — terrified of the one certainty in life. Back in Atitlán, I dreamed about my death, about how my body returned to the ground that grew the food we sold at market. My bones leached into the water that formed the lake. By that point, I was like my *bisabuelo*, with furrows plowed into sagging skin and nothing but memories of how things used to be better. I sometimes wonder if the life I'm living now, sitting on a plastic chair in a hospital waiting area watching a janitor chase invisible germs, is just the memory of the parts of me that fed the ground after my death. When you celebrate death, you see there's nothing to be afraid of.

Maybe this time, when we take our cups of tea, she won't turn on the TV. She'll look at me and we'll talk about the family that will celebrate her, and the ground that she will feed. Then I'll find a new place to live, so the money I earn flows south and all of this hasn't been for nothing.

Eduardo Lopez

I see the guy, waiting. He lifts his eyes, headphones playing something with brass. He's Hondureño, maybe Guatemalteco. Barely twenty. He's hired help, waiting for his *señora*. No one else can see us, but we see each other.

He watches out of the corner of his eye as I push the mop along the joint between the wall and the floor. That's where the dust gets trapped. That's where the microbe testers from the agency get down on their hands and knees and swab. Then they threaten you. Say that you're on thin ice unless you work the next double shift. And it's this or work in a milk shed in the middle of nowhere, wincing at the pink-raw udders and the squelch of shit mixed with straw, looking down when farmer Brice comes in swinging a shotgun and talking about the 'last guy to double cross him' and avoiding the eyes of his wife, who seems just as trapped as the animals.

A tiny buckled shoe appears in front of the mop and I dab it back into the bucket I drag like a ball and chain.

"Mister," says the shoe, "when can my Momma leave the hospital?"

I look for escape, but there's no one to save me.

The shoe is connected to the leg of a small girl, around seven or eight, with tight braids and little teeth. Her eyes dazzle through her thick-framed glasses.

"Soon, I hope." That's what I've been telling myself, but it's been nearly four years away. There's nobody to dig me out of this mess. We're just alike, this girl and I, except

I'm pushing fifty and she's not yet in middle school. "Wanna help me mop?"

She nods, and for a moment, I think she's going to clamp onto my leg and hug me. She's the same age Mia was when I left Mexico.

Now the guy with headphones looks up. He sees me.

Ruby Carson

The man with the mop didn't say anything about my jammies. Some of the hospital people did. 'Didn't anyone pack your day clothes? Where are your parents?' If I help the man with the cleaning, that woman and her clipboard woman won't bother me with questions. Questions are hard when you have to sleep on a plastic chair.

The mop's heavy. Hard to lift into the bucket. The janitor helps me squeeze it. He kind of looks like Uncle Néstor, the man Momma gives our money to. This guy would make a nicer uncle.

"I've done this before," I say.

The janitor looks at me, but he's thinking of somewhere far away.

"At home, Momma says I can take care of both of us. I brush the floor and clean the dishes." I can tell he doesn't want to ask questions. Not like the clipboard woman.

"Want a stick of gum?" he asks.

I nod. Is it mint or juicy fruit? Either one will take the hospital taste out of my mouth.

Back on my hard chair, I open the packet and fold the gum into my mouth. Fruity, just like I wanted. She should only be a few more hours. Last overdose I waited at home, out of sight of Child Services. I swear, my mom hates them more than the TV news anchor — the one she dated. And sometimes, after this, we have some good months. She tells Uncle Néstor not to come. I go to school every day.

A clipboard with a pen trapped in its jaws rests on the woman's lap next to me. I don't look up. If I close my eyes and sleep, she won't ask questions. She won't ask where I got the gum. She won't make me talk about what's wrapped in the tin foil that Uncle Néstor gives to Momma.

Kayleigh Harris

This girl is one of those kids who can sense authority — the ones who can detect any hint of broccoli ground into their spaghetti and meatballs. 'Abnormally independent' is the term we use on our incident forms. I take a breath and step into the waiting area.

The form says *Ruby Carson — abnormally independent.* Her mother has been on my radar since the incident with her dealer. She holds down a job. When she's clean, she goes to meetings and the kid goes to school. Ruby must get those smarts from somewhere. She is a smart girl.

In the hallway, she's been playing janitor. If only we could all escape tough decisions by washing the floor and squeezing a mop. I don't even have time to clean my apartment once a week.

Although I see a girl in pajamas who looks younger than her nine years, I've got to do my job. It takes hard work to reach this point. We must talk without an outcome in mind. That's the brief (which is almost impossible to follow). But I'll ask the questions and follow the protocol. That's the only way I manage to leave the heartache at work.

She eyeballs me as I sit next to her. The clipboard waits on my lap.

"Remember me?"

"How could I forget?" she replies. "Nobody else is talking to me in their fancy pantsuits."

It's not my choice to wear trousers — the department demands it.

This one may take a while. I may be here past ten am, but that's not nearly as long as that little girl's been waiting.

"I'm going to ask a few questions, Ruby. That's all."

If it's anything like last time, she'll focus harder on the answers than she would for a school midterm. She'll take her time to process the real question and the chain of reasoning that will offer me no choice but to leave her in that run-down two-bed with her addict mother. She won't agree to the audio recording. She'll look right through me as I fill in the questionnaire. Maybe she'll never trust a woman in a suit again.

Before I start, I should call Henry at the office. He'll need to know why I'm late for my next appointment.

HENRY CAUDRY

"Two cinnamon logs please, Darla. And two filter coffees."

The rest of the transaction, the small talk, the folding of a dollar bill into the tip jar, that's all autopilot. My daughter is backed into the corner, staring at a laptop plastered with stickers. Her cup's empty. She hasn't seen me yet.

My cell buzzes and it's one of the CPS agents. I'll call her back.

Molly comes here when things are not going well with her girlfriend. What was it this time? She'll refuse the donut and say she's focused on her work. Her generation has a problem with almost all normal foods now. I used to bring grilled cheese to her bedroom door after she refused to sit at the table with her mother and me. She ate it back then, but now it's 'soy this' and 'olive oil' that. At least she'll drink the coffee. Each line of code she taps into her laptop is like building a wall up one brick higher. She's twenty-six for Christ's sake.

The line moves along and I shuffle to the station for creamer and sugar. Maybe she'll eat half of my donut. Hell if I need it.

Pop music drifts from the high speakers and cars fly past on Herald Street.

At other tables, school kids squabble over phones, and workmen shoot the breeze. Two mothers park their strollers and sit.

My hands grip the plastic tray. I wave with my eyes. "Hey, honey."

She looks up and considers whether to remove the earphones.

I gauge the reaction. No eye roll. No flick of the green streak in her hair. Guess that's why I'm the mediator between Molly and her mother. Nearly two years since she came out and they still don't talk.

My hand gets the sudden urge to take out my phone and call the office. Dealing with chaos would be easier than getting my daughter to accept a coffee and a donut.

She knows I come here for my 10:30 break. What am I supposed to do, ignore her? Molly finally takes her earphones out and shuts the lid of her computer. "Dad?" she says, pointing to the door.

As I turn, the bell above the door jangles merrily and two masked gunmen breeze in.

MOLLY CAUDRY

When you're in the quietest corner of the only cafe with decent WiFi, you hope the anti-boomer anti-MAGA stickers on your laptop are enough to keep folks from disturbing you.

Then your old man walks in.

My father displays the same look a guilty dog gives its owner when pleading for a treat. Except he already has two donuts on his tray. It's the same look Janine gives me after we fight. I have to forgive one of them or I'll have no one in my corner.

The door jangles and I look up. This can't be real. My insides coil like I'm a fully primed wind-up car. Two thugs walk in, guns in hand, and the sound cuts to zero. Apart from the chirpy music. *This robbery is brought to you by Avril Lavigne.*

I remove my headphones and slowly close the lid of the Macbook.

"Dad?"

He turns and sees the picture — masks, guns, and no happy ending. Then he looks at me and mouths 'run'. At least I think that's what he means.

They say the worst thing you can do in a hostage situation is nothing. One person refuses to comply and it flips the script. I never knew that would be me.

My hand clamps the computer tight to my chest. I have a second, maybe two before these knuckle-draggers shout some stupid demands. Stand up slowly. Don't arouse suspicion. The door is wide open. The radio plays "A Thousand Years." Three cups of caffeine sting my veins and I bolt for the outside world.

The crash disturbs the air around. Gunshot. Both my feet leave the ground. I expect the punch and burn of high-velocity metal. But I land and make for the door. One step. Two. Hold your breath. My feet slap the floor like drumsticks on a tight skin. *Smack. Smack.* Who or what did they shoot? Should I look back? Why the fuck did I choose a laptop over staying with my father? The image of us, plastic guns in hand, facing the Time Crisis II machine at the arcade flashes through my mind — him, fifty pounds lighter, and me, eighteen years younger. I was always a terrible shot, and he covered me with decent marksmanship and more dollar bills.

Once you release a wind-up car it goes until the tension drains. Outside, I keep going. A hundred yards or more. I look up to a sky that goes on forever. Put more distance between you and them. What can they do, shoot and miss again?

I stand at the corner of Silverton and Waverley. I place the computer on the ground and my hands find my knees. A few deep breaths. No traffic passes. The song has been wiped off the face of the Earth and replaced by the far-away drone of combines.

When I take out my phone, I don't dial 911. Janine's number stares back at me. Calling. Calling.

Janine Bowen

My phone buzzes and buzzes. It's the third call from Molly. I told her to take the day to consider our relationship and we'll discuss it. When she gets back from wherever she goes all day. The McDonald's out on the interstate?

Text to Molly: *We both need time and space to think. Let's talk this evening.*

If last time is anything to go by, she'll get more and more dramatic, bombarding my Insta with her accusations. To escape, my feet carry me past the walls of beige cubicles, away from the chattering call handlers, past the empty coffee pot, and out into the parking lot. I'll make the time up at lunch.

The cigarette dangles from my lips, hanging on for dear life. *Damn it.* My lighter is still on my desk. She'll smell the smoke on my braids when I get home, not that I care. We're both human, I'll say. We both know we're in it together — that there will be no one else. But she'll never say it.

"Need a light?" A senior with a Betty White smile holds out her Zippo, the flame straining to reach my cigarette.

"My savior," I say.

We stand there and smoke in beautiful silence. I don't even know why she's here. Does she have something to do with the school? That patterned cardigan is not really office wear.

One last greedy draw as my cigarette burns down to the nub. I blow out the smoke and it hangs in the air in front of us.

The lady waves it away with her hand.

"Nice doing business with you," she says.

My phone buzzes. An email from Molly. As expected. But when I swipe the screen, the subject line grips me around the throat.

My eyes search for help. Anyone. I try to call the lady, but nothing comes out. She scoots round the corner toward the school.

ENID STANFORD

When I get to the kindergarten gates, Gilligan is standing on the steps with Miss Yung. His hands are jammed so far into his pockets I can't tell exactly what has happened, but I know something has happened.

The other kids are gone. A few teachers patrol the concrete, skirting garish hopscotch lines.

Miss Yung waves me through the gates. "Mrs. Stanford." She omits the word 'finally'.

I take a drag of my imaginary Davidoff slim and brace myself for his latest misdeeds. He's not a bad kid, but he's got no time with his father and very little with his mother. Both lawyers. Sometimes I draw the line at babysitting, and they pay a local girl seven twenty-five an hour to watch him. When I was young, mothers were worth much less than $7.25.

"I didn't want to have this conversation over the phone," she says. "In fact, I was hoping to speak with his parents."

I laugh. Not much chance of that. "They have their secretaries screen their calls. I can't even reach them."

She frowns and Gilligan copies her as if trying to transfer the punishment to his errant parents.

"He's biting again."

This seems to make my grandson quite angry. When I ask him why he does it, he uses a three-pronged defense: it's not fair, it was an accident, and another kid once bit him.

If only his mother and father were around, they could

teach him a thing or two about fallacies in logic and watertight defenses. Until then, he'll keep getting sanctioned.

I placate Miss Yung. One advantage of being old is that good people don't want to be rude. I'm not sure when things changed, but my daughter grew from a timid bookworm into a brazen parenting expert. She is a lot ruder than Miss Yung, who climbs down from 'musts' to 'if this happens again.'

In the car, Gilligan seethes. He plays with his too-long hair and stares without focus. On the radio, there's a news bulletin about a shooting. I switch it off and for a second, Gilligan's eyes meet mine in the rearview mirror.

His mother's office is barely a one-minute drive, but she won't leave that place. We'll go straight to her.

JOEY BROWN

A little old lady and a kid approach the desk. "Good morning, officer," she says with a voice from an elder home's daytime commercial.

I tell her I'm not an officer, but a security operative. She can probably guess the only time I use the pistol in my belt is at the firing range once a year. I don't tell her I used to draw it a lot more until they kicked me off the force. It should be my crooked partner's pension that got cut. I don't tell her I'm on fourteen an hour with shitty benefits. My greatest asset is knowing how to fix the barcode entry gates.

The grandchild wanders off and starts bothering the potted tree. He shakes it like he's got a cat by the neck.

"I'm here to see Barbara Stanford at White & Stanford."

There's no need to check the ledger or the system. "I'm afraid she's in a deposition all morning." No point ringing her either.

The lady places a liver-spotted hand on the desk, breaching the invisible shield of my brown uniform. "I figured... I'm her mother, and this is Gilligan." She looks for the kid, who is mashing the elevator buttons to no effect due to his lack of a passcode.

I tell her it doesn't matter who she is — no visitors are allowed without an appointment. This is what I say at least twenty times a day. This is why they pay me fourteen an hour. I don't tell her my wife's been looking for a job that 'works for her' for over two years. I don't tell her I go to sleep guilty and wake up tired.

Her eyes fire up. The sweet lady mutates into a silver-haired lizard with a forked tongue. Her hands claw the desk. "Mister," she hisses, "this has gone on too long. I'm going up there." She turns and snaps her fingers at Gilligan, who looks up and falls in line.

"We'll be going up to see White and Stanford." She picks up the kid with a struggle and drops him over the barrier. Then she lifts one leg over the low-barrier gate.

My shoulders stiffen and my gut sinks.

"What're you gonna do, sweetie, shoot me?"

LETICIA BROWN

I stare at the screen. *This is it. The one.* My fingers twitch like little workers eager to fire out my resume. Something stops me. What if there's a catch?

Work from your cell phone and earn up to $2000 dollars a week. No experience necessary. Attention to detail, storage space, and strong sales skills required. No initial investment — all training provided at the company's expense. Get started today!

That's the key: no startup fee. More competition to apply, but an actual opportunity at the end of it. One term to watch out for is that applicants have to 'invest in themselves'. The money I won in my accident claim went on investments — courses and starter packs. My husband makes me keep a timesheet now to show how much I make per hour.

None of this is Joey's fault. Why should a man whose family depends on food stamps have to put his body on the line for his employers?

It's all going to change now. We used to dream of a bigger house, a fancy car, a personal coach for Jackson, and hiring a landscaper. Now we dream of a trip to a baseball game, sitting behind the plate, one hot dog each, cheering the batter towards the major league. That's what we did on that horrible day Joey left the force — we ate hot dogs at the game and made love the same night. I held him while he fell asleep. Now I barely get five hours rest from worry. The meds don't work like they say.

Outside, a siren wails. I go to the window and open the blinds. Sun bursts in, and for a moment, I feel warm. But as the sound of the siren grows, my anxiety swells, drowning the sense of hope I had for this job. I don't know why. The sound grows to a scream as the car shoots down the street. My breath catches in my throat. You never know what might happen.

The noise dies and I return to the desk. No upfront cost means I can begin today. Do I even need to discuss it with my husband? I tap 'get started' on my phone screen and enter my details.

Amanda O'Rourke

"And people say women shouldn't carry a gun."

Your partner looks straight ahead and drives. "Nobody says that."

Trees shoot past like you're flying. After a few rides, you get used to the bumps and the corners. But you never forget your first shootout. That's what they say at the academy, anyway. A donut joint? How will you ever live this down? A local store owner called it in. Two perps, lots of diners.

Their car skirts the traffic and blazes through the intersections, sirens blaring. The Little O's sign grows bigger. A girl in a loose sweatshirt runs down the street. You call in the location.

It doesn't matter what you want. One sniff of adrenaline and the training kicks in. Your old man said that, and he made captain.

Davis exhales after the car comes to a halt. He reaches out and for a moment, you think he's going to lay his hand on top of yours. He doesn't do that anymore. It's not a competition, but your heart's going more than his, surely. It rises inside, wild with energy bursting to get out. For now, you say nothing. It's time. Open the door. Gear up. The parking lot feels just like the VR, but everything at the sides of your vision blurs.

They're still here. Dumbasses couldn't even split in the seven minutes it took you to arrive. You hear them before we see them, shouting at the staff. "Fucking do this. Fucking do that."

Everyone thinks you should diffuse the situation, go softly. They've never held a gun. It's fire versus fire, and cops have to make themselves big. At the end of it, humans are just animals; you fight or run. Bigger and louder shows them who the real predator is.

"Ready?" says Davis. It's a question that doesn't need answering.

He'll kick the door and you'll be first in, ready to be the loudest. Your heart feels bigger than your entire head. Your boots could knock down an Olympic wrestler.

For a second you see the reflection in the front door of Little O's Coffee and Donuts. A single red curl has escaped your cap. Kevlar vest strapped tight and a PD service weapon in your right hand. The reflection is three inches taller than the real-life Amanda O'Rourke.

"Go!"

Nadia Belhadj

Andre said it was a one-time thing, but here we are again. Robbers always go back for one more. We're not desperate, but he's right — we don't have much choice.

Andre told me to wear loose-fitting, black clothes. Gloves and a mask too. It's hot and the material scratches like a *hammam* loofah. He said I'm the only one smart enough to keep my mouth shut. Literally, no words. Under all those black layers, no one suspects a quiet Muslim girl.

So far, we got the register, and Andre's taking every last wallet and purse. My muscles twitch in readiness. I run track at the community college but a race is nothing compared to the high of fleeing with a bag of money clutched to your chest.

The diners look back like our mere presence hurts them. They take an age to hand over cash and valuables. Some of them begin to argue and *smash*, I crack the counter with the butt of my replica. The teen server flinches and goes to stand under the tinny speaker.

He shoots a glance at me. *Stay vigilant.* There's no point in this if we can't pay off the debt. Andre, Andre's kid brother, and his aging grandfather are only family I've got since my father's crash.

Last time it finished quick. Point, ping, open, cash, shut, out. We screamed and laughed all the way onto the freeway. It took hours for the adrenaline to settle. This time, something sucked all the air out of my chest and I've been itching ever since. It happened right after that girl ran out and right before the gun went off. I can't look at the guy on the floor. He'll make it, won't he?

Each cough or mutter sounds louder than the shot. I can't feel my feet under me. Hot sweat runs the track between my shoulder blades.

Then the wail of the squad car arrives from nothing. It's not like the movies where they hear it five minutes away. Tires screech in the lot. One, two pairs of boots. Guns drawn. Barking orders.

We have to split. Now!

I wish I could say it aloud. Scream it. But I can't.

Andre's wide eyes travel across the entire diner. He cocks his gun and motions to me. *Back door, Nadia. Go.*

Harry Katar

"This is the friendly visit," I say to the old-timer at the door. One Sidney Greene. My knuckles are itching.

Of course, he has no clue about the loan. They never do. He stands with his hand on the door like he could stop me, at six-five and two-fifty, from running right over the top of him.

There is no negotiation, even though they try. That's why the firm recruits ex-military like me. All the grayscale has been beaten out of us by years of protocols. Once you've seen bone grinding through a quadricep or a missing hand in the dirt, a few bruises are nothing. A good soldier is a robot; a good collection agent follows strict protocol. This is my protocol:

Do not enter into negations or answer questions.

During the friendly visit, clearly state the amount owed, the collection date, and the precise physical consequences of non-compliance.

In the case of non-compliance ensure that you are not filmed or seen carrying weapons. Ensure your hands and arms remain unmarked. Use an unimpeachable alibi.

Bodily damage must be debilitating but not permanent.

Some of the guys in my company weren't resilient. Only people wired a certain way can truly circumnavigate doubt. We learned about the tribes of Helmand and the fluid nature of their relationship with the Taliban. Their debt and honor. Those people were just as likely to die from a lack of medical centers as from a misplaced airstrike. But they only hold grudges against flags and uniforms.

People who take out high-interest loans don't like uniforms either. These are people who can't follow society's norms. But if you focus on what is real, what cannot be changed, you don't need rules and regulations. That's why I paint still life. The better you get, the closer to reality you are. A bowl of fruit is always a bowl of fruit.

During the doorstep conversation, points one and two are followed to the letter. The old man's hands shake when he shuts the door. He says something about his grandson coming up with a big score soon. I zip my jacket and walk back to the car. I'll be back here in three days. I can feel it. When I get back to the apartment tonight, my hands hold the brush steady, and I'll paint reality.

Ray Greene

When we learned about game theory in math, they made it sound cool. Right and wrong are just statistics. Be cool and calculated. Be Tom Brady. But real-life decisions don't follow neat patterns, even if these end-of-year speeches say they do.

I sat there in class, looking at the calculations, thinking that the outcome is win or lose, not life or death. Blue Cross has lawyers. When you can't pay a $22,000 bill because they made you take a DNA test to prove the cardholder is not a blood relation, when they say the medication costs have to increase because of the latest global crisis, when you work every spare minute busing tables at IHOP (and that money pays for your step-grandfather's meds), then you don't have a lawyer on speed dial. Lawyers cost more than 22k.

Then, the insurers still take the house. You have nowhere to stay but your car.

Your friends in the sports hall don't consider those variables. They just get to be Tom Brady, sitting in the pocket, holding the money, waiting for the receivers to run their routes.

The white teeth sitting around me babble about summer parties and college. Their gums are red as the payment letters shoved through our door.

Whatever my brother's plan to fix this is, Andre's going to make decisions that lie outside the realms of a theoretical test. People like us have it impossible.

When the principal comes on stage ready to close out the year, the rest of them go wild. For them, it's the end. I've got summer classes to finish up the year and get my diploma. And if Andre doesn't come through, I'll have to quit and go full-time. Can restaurants pay you less if you don't get your diploma?

Principal Joyce

We did the right thing, leaving the keynote for Coach Primley. He's quite articulate. He speaks 'teenager'. Who needs to hear another 'rousing' speech from a tired principal? Yes, there is news — war, social media, politics, the planet, racism — but the link to this place is tenuous.

I watch Primley up there, all five feet seven of him. You don't have to be tall to be a titan. As he talks, the vein in his neck tenses like he's unable to detach the emotion of the hundreds of wins and losses celebrated and suffered in this gym.

Another year through. Yes, the district reports will come in, and budgets will be cut, but it's over, and we didn't crumble into dust. We made it another twelve months. Sometimes I think high school is becoming a more unrealistic long-term career than playing in the NBA.

This must be the first time ever that the whole bunch of them are silent. No shuffling, no phone screens connected to eyes.

I'm interested to ask Primley if it's all been worth it — the years of struggle. The poor man coming back after what happened to his wife. He's adaptable if anything. I can't imagine trying to connect up all the reasons he continued. As he speaks, a whole lifetime blows out like steam escaping a kettle.

I am fond of this place, but each semester, the brightness of students fades along with the paintwork. My aim is to get out in under five years. I'll spend the days in my workshop and I won't come out until I've made a good set of oak chairs and a dinner table.

Coach Primley trails off mid-sentence. It's unlike him to finish on a low. He stumbles and reaches for the lectern. It's a cheap hardboard thing and topples just as he does. He grips his chest. The whole hall gasps as one.

The second that passes before his head hits the floor of the very court he's patrolled for thirty-two years is a long and awful slow-motion replay. We watch the last ball drift high through the air, searching for the three, game clock at zero. It bounces off the rim with a horrible smack and Primley drops to the floor.

DURING

Coach Primley

"I ain't going to keep you long. You know me — man of many words on the court and few words off it."

Undivided attention is what a coach expects, but he rarely gets it. Three hundred pairs of eyes concentrate their gaze. I'm an ant under the magnifying glass, but heat only makes me stronger.

"In a game, the final minute can last five or even ten. Timeouts, restarts, fouls. Time doesn't run as normal. This talk is going to be that last minute for me." My throat swells like there's a golf ball in there. "I..."

The air in the hall turns static. The smell of polish and sweat turns to burnt toast. It fires my nostrils. How could you lose your place? You practiced the speech enough damn times.

My mind flashes to tomorrow. I'm outside, sipping iced tea, listening to the neighborhood live, reading a newspaper with a blurred headline.

"I just need to share something with you." The words ooze out like treacle.

"It's everything I learned wrapped up in a minute, and don't worry—" My right knee buckles and I stagger. Gripping the lectern, I manage to right myself and brush my shirt, as if a speck of dust or a food stain knocked me over. Can't let whatever this is stop me. "Sorry about... I ain't gonna tell you to work hard, or believe in yourselves or any of that bullcrap."

Then it hits me like a hot wrench driven into my chest. I gasp. "I think—". The faces in front of me are just big eyes and fast heartbeats. It's the same faces as the proud relatives uniting in hope that the high ball drops into the net. The high ball hardly ever drops into the net.

The wrench twists and my ribs burn like they're meat seared on an oil-drum grill. I can hear the scorch of flesh. If I could take just one single breath, I'd laugh. All these sixty years to tell kids to count on each other, and they're all watching like helpless pieces of fruit in a bowl.

Now the smell of polish and sweat returns. No life flashing before me, but that piece of advice I didn't give echoes in my mind. Perhaps the principal will have to give some kind of speech after all. Perhaps next year, the team will win state, all in memory of Coach Primley. The vice that grips my heart tightens half-turn by half-turn. Darkness peeks the corners of my eyes. A commotion. Shoes squeak the floor. I feel hands on me. I wonder if there is time for them to bring the machine. The paddles. The clock ticks down toward zero. Always down to zero.

Kyle Radley

"We've got to be quick, Kyle." Even though no one can hear us in the girls' bathroom, she hiss-whispers the words.

There's a storm inside. It's been there ever since what happened with Jayden, testing every corner for weak spots. Sometimes I think it won't hold. Just keep quiet. Maybe Hayley won't say what you think she's going to say.

She has a couple of strands of carefully straightened hair that draw your eye down to her waist. When she wants something, she smoothes them between her fingers. This girl stands about a foot shorter than me, but it's me who feels smaller.

"I did the test and it came back with two lines."

Those two parallel lines extend years into the future. They go on forever. Arguments over dinner, fighting to make rent on a high-school salary, and joint custody getting in the way of everything I was set to accomplish. Goodbye to college ball. While I follow the lines, that storm builds. All I can say is "What does two lines mean?"

"You're gonna be a father." She ain't whispering now.

Miss Brinkley says I'm a better writer than I know. She knows it's easier to write down all the things I want to say to my asshole father than to say them. Not that I send the letters. There's no way out of this. Abandoning a kid at 17 weeks is way worse than 17 years. I'll tell Hayley it's not her; it's me. And it's Jayden. I'll tell her it's two teammates destined to go to different colleges, wondering if one kiss means they're gay. They'll follow their own lives, two lines extending out for years, fighting it, never able to come together. Sure, they will feel the lightning shoot through their thumbs when they text, but most of those texts will remain unsent. That's the way the storm stays inside. And I want to tell her all of this as we stand in front of the mirrors, two seventeen-year-olds, keeping their ears tuned to the principal's words in the gym.

All that comes out is, "But we only did it once."

Roger Radley

In prison, a break from reality goes like this: a talk in an airless room sitting at a steel desk with a lawyer who would look more at home in front of a kindergarten class than in a courtroom.

"I'm afraid, Mr. Radley, the offer remains the same."

The judge gave me five years; the state said it would be one if I gave up the crypto keys. In reality, everything is for sale, including the length of custodial sentences. The United States Government is truly terrified of people having control over their own money. If that's the only terror they have to deal with, they've got it easy compared to me.

"I thought the new email chain we found would collapse the case." Did I accumulate funds from investors? Yes. Was I told de facto by the SEC that it was, at that point, legal to store portfolios on blockchain ledgers? Yes. Did they attempt to delete those messages? Yes.

She looks at me with a weariness I haven't seen before. "We are certain the conviction will be quashed on appeal. The state is playing for time. It could be a year before the hearing."

I touch my swollen ribs and tell her I don't have twelve months left. When you look into the whites of another inmate's eyes, all you see is time.

She tells me she's sorry. She wishes the system worked better than 'pay to play'. What do I value more, she asks, my family and my life or five million dollars? She doesn't know money is the only way I can pay back the years of lies. No woman deserves to be chained to a man they could never please because only men can please him.

"You look kind of tired," I say.

She chokes down a lump in her throat. What comes out is a strange little sob. "I'm not..." she doesn't finish.

Before she stands to go, she takes a breath and we both realize how little air there is in the consultation room. She doesn't babble anything about another strategy, the next court date, or even give me a perky ditto to keep my head down. She knows white-collar guys like me end up with nothing.

"Goodbye, Miss Schwarz," I say.

Then she leaves.

Catherine Schwarz

We're deep into it. 'The conversation'. That one argument from which there is no going back.

Peter said if I ever want a baby, I should do as he says. No questions. Ever. He said fights and divorces would be a bad look for a woman who might run for judge one day. How can I expect to reach those heights if I can't convince my middle-aged client to trade his money for his life?

My husband looks at me, lifting a head too heavy for his body, an infant, able to focus for just a second. He smiles like he's made some masterful closing argument when in reality, he slurred his words and failed to brush the food stain from the back of his pants.

We both just stand there in the kitchen, wondering who is going to be first to call time on this five-year ordeal. Water in the pan bubbles, waiting to scald the spaghetti.

I really tried this time, but he came in guns blazing about some meaningless spat with a colleague. Why should I take his side? I know he's not easy to work with.

The phone rings. It's a corded one, attached to the wall, and there's only one person who actually calls it.

"Don't you fucking dare pick up." His mouth foams as he spits out the words. And he thought I was going to rule in his favor, cuddle up and say "You were right, darling. I should do everything you say."

It's been a while since I really wanted to speak to my mother. She has perfect timing, I'll give her that.

The ringing infiltrates our heads like a morning alarm clock.

He puts his arm across and blocks my path.

I never lose my cool; that's what really riles him. When he punches a wall or grabs my throat, he can't blame it on self-preservation. He's not a big man, my husband, but he's got a kind of coiled strength.

My arm reaches past him for the receiver and he shoves my chest. My breath whistles out and I fly backward, just managing to stay upright. My hip smacks the edge where the worktop joins the cabinet. I ignore the pain.

The phone rings on. She won't hang up.

Then, before I can tell him to leave, to go without packing, it's over, it's over, a waste of five good years, so get the fuck out of my house, and don't come back, he snatches a kitchen knife from the rack. My shoulders arch and my mind flies too fast to process anything as speech. But he turns, marches over to the phone, and hacks the cord, slicing back and forth with the knife, like he's wanted this for years and he's glad I'm watching.

The hairs on my arms stand straight up and my hip throbs with each stolen breath.

Finally, the ringing stops.

BETH SCHWARZ

And now the line's gone dead. Perfect. I'll have to call her cell.

Manny looks at me like I'm sick in the head.

"I'm just calling my daughter is all."

Rectal cancer can ruin anyone, especially a lady of my age. But sharing news that will hurt your child, the one constant in your whole adult life, that's what really tears up your insides.

Before I can take a breath and prepare myself to deliver the same news I got from the doctor, the phone in my hand goes off. It startles me and I almost fumble it.

Manny brings a cup of chamomile tea.

"Can you put some sugar in it?" I ask. "What's it going to do? Kill me?"

When I answer the phone I can tell something's wrong. Catherine's in that turtle mode, not offering a word more than she needs to. Lawyers can be like that. It sounds like she's outside, walking the neighborhood streets.

"Is it Peter or the job?"

She says it's her husband. "I think this time it's…"

Keeping quiet used to work. It used to make her open up. This time, she just leaves her car-crash marriage on show — a severed limb hanging by sinew. Eventually, she says "What did you want to tell me so bad?"

The sugared tea is now sitting on the table next to my left arm. The *Wheel of Fortune* intro rolls on the television and my mind spins in primary colors, slowly coming to settle on an option. My right arm holds the phone and my mouth doesn't move. I can barely breathe, let alone tell her the news. The steam from the tea bathes my arm and I imagine how sweet my first sugar in eighteen months will taste.

"Manny's gonna need a new job," I say. My voice comes out surprisingly level. Even. "It's stage four."

What can you say to that? Should I have given her the vowels and asked her to guess the phrase?

"You still there, Catherine?"

I imagine her sitting on the sidewalk outside her white-picket prison, just like she used to do as a teenager, needing her space but reluctant to leave the safety of home to get up to mischief with her school friends because she didn't want me to sit and steam on my own. Over the silence of the line between us, the put-put of a sprinkler plays the same cadence as the wheel when it's coming to a final decision.

I tell her I'm off the meds. I tell her I'm drinking sweet tea for the first time in two years. "What's it gonna do?" I say, "Kill me?"

She doesn't laugh.

When I tell her to come over, she says she needs space to think.

A sigh escapes into the mouthpiece of the phone. "I'm sorry. Don't think I could have said the words if we were in front of each other."

After she hangs up, I drink my tea. Manny and I watch *Wheel of Fortune* but the contestant doesn't win much at all.

Manuel Hernández

Mrs. Schwarz tells me she is going to die soon. I guess it's not a surprise, but still.

She tells me in the Uber on the way home. The driver pretends not to listen to her as she talks out the side of her mouth. At least he will get a story out of it. I'm not even permitted to drive in this country. I only received my Guatemalan license a couple of years back, but one traffic stop and I'm out. *En serio.*

"Lo siento mucho, señora," I say.

She says she's glad she can flush the pills down the toilet. They already make both of us feel sick.

We sit there, *en silencio,* holding hands for the rest of the ride home. The car crawls along, passing shops where workers get a pay stub with tax deductions, and houses where families park their SUV on the drive. The sun shines bright orange and the lawns glow extra green. I never learned how people make gardens look pretty. I attack the grass with the weed wacker each week, so the neighbors think I'm just another Latino landscaper.

There is this brick living in my stomach. It's been there since I realized I couldn't go back. Mrs. Schwarz has a brick in her stomach too, only hers is black and made of cancer. Sometimes I hate the brick, wish I could throw it through the windshield of the Lincoln that rusts in the garage. Just as I think this, the sound of a siren grows and I instinctively sit a little straighter.

"You gonna go back to your folks in Guatemala?" she asks.

My body lurches as if it is deciding for me that it's time to return. It's like how your legs walk you toward the grill on the street because it's a childhood memory that comes to life every time you smell roasted corn. But however strong the pull, my legs will stop at the *frontera*. "I'm not sure, Mrs. Schwarz," I say.

The driver turns and asks which house it is.

Mrs. Schwarz says, "The one with the ugly-ass lawn."

This makes me laugh and her wheeze.

The car pulls up to the drive and the relief of being home washes me clean.

I open the car door to hoist her out and she looks me good in the eye and says, "You're gonna need a new job soon, Manny."

Eduardo Lopez

13:04: Eduardo
Just to let you know, this will be my last day.

13:04: Rubicon Cleaning:
Please call the office. We would like to discuss this
with you.

13:05: Eduardo
I won't be doing that. This is my last day.

13:06: Rubicon Cleaning:
missed call

13:08:
missed call

Can you pick up the phone? We'd like to offer you
improved compensation.

13:11: Eduardo
Still below minimum though. Right? I'm leaving
town.

13:15: Rubicon Cleaning:
Employees must give two weeks notice period to
allow the agency to organize cover.

Your last paycheck will be withheld unless you
work the two weeks.

13:27:
There is still time to change your mind. We are a
family at Rubicon, and don't want any employees
to get into any trouble with the law.

13:28

> *missed call*

13:29

> Answer your damn phone!

13:45

> We give you months of work and this is how you
> repay us?

After that, I switch it off. Working for those *cabrones* is mutually assured destruction. I stay and I'm trapped. They call ICE and I squeal.

I take the time to compose the message I've wanted to send for three years. *Amor. Papi está de vuelta.*

There's a million other sentences I've cut. Those are the ones I bear so that Mia doesn't have to. Now I have to figure out how I can make it home with only one hundred seventy-eight dollars and a half tank of gas.

No point in finishing the shift now. I rest the mop against the doors and wonder if that little girl will pick it up when she comes out of her mother's hospital room.

Ruby Carson

"Hey there. Ruby, ain't it?"

Listen to this woman, saying 'ain't', even though she looks like a walking Sears catalog. Maybe if I don't confirm my name she'll leave.

"We have permission to speak with you, ok? Your mother—"

"Who's we?" I ask. "You're only one person, *ain't* you?"

She fumbles a bit after that. Tells me something about Child Protective Services and how everyone has rights.

I know my momma is no angel. You get used to being hungry, doing the grown-up jobs, and caring for her when she's sick. You get used to lying and running circles around government agencies.

This woman is one I've spoken to before. She recognized me when she came in, I know. The chewing gum the janitor gave me has lost its flavor and I want to put it under the chair so some unsuspecting person touches the grossness. At the school fundraiser last year they had a mystery box filled with worms which turned out to be spaghetti. *That* was gross. I couldn't go this year.

The pointy-elbowed lady writes something down on her clipboard. She told me her name, but it goes into the box of things I don't think about. "If you don't answer my questions," she says, "we'll have to visit your house."

That will mean a lot of cleaning and tidying on my part. "I'm just taking my time."

She asks me about school. I tell her I get sick and have to stay home sometimes, but I always catch up on the homework. She asks me a lot of questions about my momma, about what she does and how she treats me. The answer to most of these questions is yes, but when I say 'no', the lady looks into my eyes to find the real answer.

I'm so tired. Why won't she leave? Once we get home I can escape the *bing-bong* announcements and the chemical smell.

"No, I'm not hungry. No, I don't need a ride. No, Momma's friend is waiting. No, it's a holiday, so school's closed." The answers tumble out of my mouth.

Finally, the lady gets off the plastic seat and crouches down in front of me. Close up, her face is big. She says I can call her any time. She is so close I can smell the shampoo she uses. She doesn't look like a clipboard anymore. I see the lines on her forehead just how you notice paper isn't flat if you hold it real close to your eye. Then she says, "I lost my own child, and here I am, thirteen years later—" and turns away. I don't hear the rest of what she says.

Maybe she came from a neighborhood like mine.

She reaches out and touches my hand. Hers is soft like those towels Momma took from the hotel. Maybe I'm tired, but it feels like a long time passes. Then she hands me a business card and leaves, her heels clip-clopping the hospital floor. I look at the card and don't know if I should tear it up or lock it up tight.

Then my eyes start to water and they don't stop. My sleeve gets wet through. I get hiccups from jerking up and down. The juicy fruit taste has changed to salt and saliva. The janitor has left his mop and gone. My hand hurts and I realize it's clamped around a crumpled business card.

Kayleigh Harris

We sit in the hospital corridor, her chewing on a piece of gum, acting twice her age. Ruby's hair is itching to burst out of those braids, but it somehow stays in check, just below the level required to tick it as unkempt or unhygienic. Her monosyllabic answers to my questions do the bare minimum to avoid non-compliance.

Every shift on the plastic seats emits a sound like we're on a creaking vessel. There's a young man listening to music farther down. My stomach churns and washes the remnants of the breakfast burrito I grabbed on the way here. I shouldn't be using the drive-through, but what else am I going to eat? It's not like I'm a regular at Whole Foods Market.

"Have you ever felt unsafe when this Uncle Néstor visits your mother?"

She says he's OK. He's never made her feel unsafe. The cuts and bruises on the mother's face tell a different story.

"Do you want some examples of things that count as unsafe?" Living in a basement with no heating system, so the damp feeds into a baby's lungs in winter (no matter how many blankets her teenage mother wraps her in). That counts as unsafe. I should know.

She chews and looks over as a porter pushes a horizontal patient through the double doors. This action knocks a loose mop to the floor. It clatters in protest and the guy with headphones looks up.

I try to keep my emotions in check these days. Go through the questions, gently push, then hold back. My therapist told me I should tell my story to the folks I work with. She said their understanding is my forgiveness.

Ruby doesn't know her mother is pregnant. It's unlikely she'll pass the necessary checks on home visits unless she has a registered partner.

Bile rises in my stomach. It's not the burrito, it's that feeling that today is not the day I sit back and tick the sheet. This girl's too smart for her own good, and she's tricking herself, just like I have for the last thirteen years.

Ruby passes the test and there are no more questions to ask.

"Do you want to know a secret about me?"

She shrugs.

I never thought I'd outpour my trauma to a child who won't understand. Or maybe she will. Here goes. "Well, it's hard not to care about your situation. I lost my own child." My throat virtually closes shut as the scene floods back. "A woman like me put her in a safe place because I couldn't care for her." I tell her I don't know where my daughter is, but I still fight for her every day.

Her eyes widen like the story is going straight in.

"Your mother is not fighting for you, Ruby, and you deserve better."

I just about make it through without my voice breaking.

She nods. After that, the invisible shutters come down over her eyes again. Nothing.

"We're out of time," I say. Then I give her a card and walk. If she's smart, she'll call. That's what I'll tell my boss anyway.

HENRY CAUDRY

The thing they don't tell you about a robbery is all your senses blend into one. It's spiritual in a way. Imagine fighting against the ocean that pulls you down after a big-wave wipeout. That's the feeling.

I take a slow step back so I can see the robbers out my left eye and Molly to my right. The gunman shouts something at Darla and the rest of the cafe sits bolted to their chairs, hands on the table, good little lambs. The construction guys and the mothers with babies, their senses shrink into one too. The place feels the size of my old station wagon.

Molly looks up. Through the thick-framed spectacles and dark makeup, her eyes try to tell me something. Fathers can read their daughters better than they can read themselves. This time is different. She seems slower, like she's still processing whether to take the route of least resistance. We talk about that a lot at CPS. An easy win is still a win.

The taste of cinnamon sugar stings my lips, Darla's tip-jar smile, the imaginary shuffling of thumbs on phones, percolating coffee, cold blood in my veins, the shallow breaths of everyone in this place, the thick air, and the ever-ringing jangle of the doors when these two came in. All one.

Molly snatches her sticker-strewn computer and dashes for the door.

My sense heightens. This is not the path of least resistance.

The taller one turns, teeth baring through the ski mask. His hand grips the pistol tight. Looks like a small caliber weapon. "Hey," he shouts, but my girl doesn't look back. She skips the five paces to freedom. Almost before he does it, I see his bony arm raise.

My legs carry me over as if a non-existent referee blew for the start of the scrimmage, and I'm hell-bent on breaking the QB's ribs. *Make the hit.* Make sure your daughter runs free, deal with her problems yourself and remember the feeling the next time you set down a cup of coffee in front of her.

We don't collide, the gunman and I. There's a sound — the impact of a crash. I fall to the floor. Pain and joy all at once. Molly gets out the door and runs without looking back.

When I put my hand to my belly, it comes up red.

MOLLY CAUDRY

Five. Four. Three. Two. One. Zero.

Five. Four. Three. Two. One—

Five. Four. How many times can you count down to zero? Janine says this helps, but how?

"Ma'am, are you still there?"

The dispatcher's voice grips me by the collar and pulls me out of the downward-draining spiral.

"Yes…" Even if the cops are quick, they won't stop them. By the time they arrive, they'll be gone.

My father and everyone else in the place are not dead. They're like that cat in the box, which is alive and dead. I heard shots. Not just one. They didn't aim for me. I mean, I was two yards from the guy.

Little O's is not like one box though. The realities of what happened have splintered off into a million different boxes; in some timelines everyone is healthy and in others, a single bullet pierces the heart of every person in that place. Guns shoot out a million possibilities, none of them as good as a misfire. Five. Four. Three. Two. One.

"Thank you for sharing that information with us. The officers are on their way." She sounds like my high school teacher. Maybe that's what high school teachers do now, moonlight by taking 911 emergency calls.

I slump down to the curb. The asphalt is searing hot even though I've been standing out of the shade all this time. Something hard presses against my chest, and I realize I've hugged the MacBook to my ribs this whole time.

Useless code bleeds into me while someone else spills their guts on the cafe floor. Who cares if the program I just wrote died? What will my clients say when I get a doctor's note for PTSD and pass the project off to a colleague? I've forgotten where I was in the count — five or four. The air tastes of gas and electricity.

"Should I stay on the line?" I say, in a cracked voice.

Back in high school my report cards always had a 'but'. An A minus, (the minus was for attitude). Maybe that's why Janine and I fit together. She got bad grades, but everyone liked her. She's got this kind of customer-service intelligence.

The lady at 911 says I can go, but I asked if I can stay on the line a minute more, just until I hear the cop cars arrive. That way, all the fragments of reality exist. In one of those millions of boxes, I have an accepting family. Janine's in there too.

I count time and finally the squad car flashes past. When it does, my legs take me after it. I walk, jog, run in pursuit. My Macbook lies deserted on the sidewalk.

JANINE BOWEN

My Fucking Dad is Dead. Pick Up!

That's the subject line. It takes a millisecond to process, but it changes my next six months, a year even. Just like that, our argument seems stupid. And I'm sitting back here at my desk with the call waiting light flashing red. On the other end of the telephone, there's probably a scared little lady worried about the co-pay on her husband's dementia care, or a corporate bosshole trying to squeeze every last dime out of the insurance quote. On the other end of the email is broken love.

Why didn't I pick up when I was on my break? I could have at least found out what happened. Heart attack? I mean the guy does not follow his doctor's diet. I let out a sigh that's a little too loud. The alarm light on my phone flashes. More than 30 seconds since the call was put through — that's an infraction (not a write-up, but it can lead to one). From across the office, the bosshole catches my eye. That's his job, to pace up and down cubicleville like a jailer swinging his keys, daring the inmates to backtalk.

I pick up the call. "Rose Health Insurance quotes department. My name is Janine and I'll be helping you today."

Maybe I can get to the bathroom after this call. Pull the 'time of the month' card. I mean, I don't like to abuse it, but there's no way to call Molly without it. However her parents treated us over the last two years, the guy should not be going so early. What was he, fifty-one? And he was Molly's only hope of coaxing her mother out of that cult of a church.

"Hello? Am I on hold or what?"

"Sorry, Ma'am," I say. I decide to go straight for the rock-bottom offer. Take that, boss man.

Then I put her on hold and write back to Molly.

Baby. I'm so sorry. If I answer, it'll be strike three. I can't. My shift ends in ninety minutes. I'll see you then. Big love.

As I hit send, the love travels through the digital airwaves, unencumbered by the stale air in the callhouse prison. To think I traded that call for a silent cigarette break with Betty White makes my skin itch.

ENID STANFORD

We will be seeing my daughter whether she likes it or not. I lift Gilligan over the entry-code barrier; he weighs a lot more than I expected. He looks back then scrambles towards the elevator. When you can't lift your grandson, he's either gotten too fat or you've gotten too old.

Bending the rules is the only thrill this old woman gets. Taking handfuls of creamer from the club to use at home, parking in the disabled spot because you are 'disabled enough' even though you don't have the badge. No one argues with a sweet old lady. Apart from this one guy.

I'm standing there in this mirror-sheen lobby. Too much marble and too much echo. I get my other leg over the barrier and walk serenely to the stairs.

"Stop!"

My heart jumps a little. All those years ago, driving away on the back of Vince's motorcycle — that made my blood run.

"Stop. I am authorized to restrain you." Rent-a-cop stands and squeezes himself out of the gap between his seat and the grand white desk.

I quicken towards the stair door. Don't look back.

Then *Whiplash*. Like I've been rear-ended by an eighteen-wheeler. I'm on the floor before I can breathe.

His breeze block hands press the weight of a piano into my back. I stare at the low table one inch from my face. Could have knocked my eyes right out of my skull. How can this be happening in my own daughter's office? My right hip screams but my mouth has nothing smart to say.

Finally, he releases his weight and asks if I am all right.

I gasp air. Check myself for breakages. Injuries at my age are no joke. I manage to get onto all fours.

"Grandma," says Gilligan, appearing next to me with his hands clamped to his sides in a 'good boy' pose, "You said it was okay."

"We didn't break any rules." My voice is hoarse.

The security guard has put himself between me and the stairs, between me and my high-powered daughter, Gilligan's mother, the only one who can straighten this out. Slowly, painfully, I get to my feet and glare at the guard. I think about asking him to call my daughter again, but he points to the open gate and the lobby doors.

Sunlight powers in.

The lobby echoes in silence. That's about how popular corporate lawyers are.

Gilligan follows the man's finger and walks into the street. "Come on, Grandma," he says.

Instead of hissing legal threats at the moron who tackled the partner's mother to the ground, I simply point at him. *Your job,* I think. *Your job.*

JOEY BROWN

There is a lot of reading to do when you are a security guard. You have to know the legal implications. Now imagine if it was a lawyer's office that wrote the dos and don'ts. Well, I read it all, followed it to a T, but here I am standing between an intruder and the stairs to the office. My shirt feels like it is two sizes too small. The playbook doesn't say anything about family members, and the woman I hauled down was a senior.

I'm a big guy, but minimal force was used. I went through every stage of de-escalation, before getting physical. The video will show that. The verbal warnings, the direct commands. She doesn't look injured. Why am I sweating?

My hands fidget in want of something to do. I wish I could undo the top button on my collar, take off the clip-on tie, or use five minutes outside. Saying anything would be wrong — apologizing, giving her more instructions to turn around and get out. All of that gives her more reason to get me fired. As if I have a chance.

When there is enough media attention on a case, someone's head has to roll. The cash in my locker was the repayment of a loan to a buddy. I didn't care where my partner got it from. Until it was internal investigations asking. How many times can circumstances beat a guy down? At least this time, there'll be no press. I might lick my wounds in peace.

My arm raises itself and points to the exit. *Get out of here. Don't make this worse.* The kid gets it. He tells grandma to meet him outside as she picks herself up.

She points at me, which is somehow worse than hurling cuss words. She'll take my job all right. What is it with people in this country wanting to take your job? I'll find the fourteen bucks an hour somewhere else, but health insurance... When did we become this spiteful?

I haven't drunk in years, but my hands rattle in want of a glass. Take a breath. Remember the playbook. Remember the video. Call upstairs. They'll suspend you. Look for a job. Call Leticia to explain. Start again, just like you did after leaving the force. It's not the end. It's just another speed bump.

LETICIA BROWN

Everyone knows about the Caramucci flea market — a yard full of old furniture, and buried in the middle, a tiny office. I'm here for money. It's not a loan. I'll earn it back twofold with this job. I've told myself that, and it's what I'll tell Joey too.

I park the car and skirt the rusting bed frames in the lot. I should be out before collecting Jackson from practice. The door to the construction cabin office is ajar.

Inside, Antonia Caramucci sits behind a mountain of desk papers. No AC. No fan. Power tools propped against one wall. It's like a pizza oven, only melamine white. What kind of person could work like this? My dread kicks up a notch.

"You're Officer Brown's wife, right?" The air carries words thick with her Italian accent and stale smoke. She looks down at the paperwork again.

He told me about his gambling problem. Baseball games. Now he trusts me with his paycheck. Now he's doing better. "He's not on the force anymore, Mrs. Caramucci."

She stops writing and stuffs the pen under her springy gray hair. "Are you working?" My eyes shift to the sledgehammer resting against the corner wall. Deliberate, surely.

I tell her that's what the money's for. It's to gain membership into an exclusive selling club. "The products I get are worth twice what I need."

"What do you need?"

There are too many answers to that question — a coach for Jackson so he's got a shot at the minor leagues, a job for Joey that won't cost his life and will pay the bills, some leads for my sales pipeline, thirty days clear of anxiety so I can hit my target, for the car to keep going on one tank of gas, for the landlord to get off our back, for all that we've put in to pay back. "An investment of two thousand."

She says she's not investing in anything. I am. She prints off some papers for me to sign. "Repayment of five hundred a week, starting next month."

I nod, but it doesn't feel like me nodding. It's fear.

She gets up and goes to the door. "Francesco!" she shouts. She'll collect the money and return in a few minutes, she says. "Sign the contract. Every page."

My hand trembles as I scrawl signature after signature on the papers, just as it does on my weekly medical expense forms. The sledgehammer in the corner of the room morphs into a Louisville Slugger. Top quality, latest design with a set of gloves and a training pigeon. Jackson is going to freak. He'll ask about the money, but he won't listen to the answer. We all prefer not to know. We all prefer not to think of consequences. We all prefer not to involve the law.

When she returns, Mrs. Caramucci says, "Some idiot shot up Little O's. We own part of that." She raises her painted-on eyebrows as if I should console her loss.

Fear usually drips in, little and often, but this is like a wave. "Oh dear," I say, wringing my hands. At least Jackson's school is in the other direction. So is the sports store. I pick up the papers to leave and sweat from my hands bleeds into the contract.

AMANDA O'ROURKE

Question: Where are the perps and what are they packing?

Answer: One at the back exit (gun could be a replica). The other is strutting around like a peacock on speed (gun is a gangland peashooter).

Question: How will they respond to direct orders or the escalation of aggression?
a) Losing conviction and transferring power to the cops
b) Unaffected
c) By matching their own increase in aggression
Answer: c)

Question: Is the fat guy slumped next to the counter wounded or dying?

Answer: That depends on how long this takes. He's pretty quiet.

Question: Has your partner recognized the need to stall for backup so they can cover the back door?

Answer: No. He has given an ultimatum to the gunman. He cares more about glory than protecting a partner who was once more than a partner.

Question: If any of the twenty-something people get into the crossfire, will your gun take the blame?

Answer: You won't even get a shot away before the guy pops you. He's got the sight advantage. Hope the kevlar will do its job.

Question: Why has nobody turned off that plinky-plinky music? And whatever happened to rock and roll?

Answer: Tell the one at the back counter to turn the music off. Shout loud from behind the entrance wall.

The ski mask nods and turns it off. Good. Now you hear the tension. It sounds like the slow tear of an infinite piece of paper. You also notice the outline of nails under the slender gloved hands. A female perp. Women never dream this stuff up; they only go along with abusive partners.

Question: Why would this dude point his gun at the female cop? According to what every other no-good thinks, women are more likely to go easy on you.

Question: Are you having a good time?

Answer: It's impossible to tell. Time has stopped and your body is weightless.

Question: Will she get away?

Answer: His accomplice already left out the other door. Backup didn't arrive, so she's gone.

Question: Did the bullet hit you before or after you got a shot away?

Answer: You are almost falling before you hear it. Your hand is on your neck, and you drop to your knees and roll in the sugar crumbs on the checkered floor. The linoleum swallows you. Warm red filling oozes through your fingers. Your windpipe burns.

Question: How many of the shots Davis fired have hit him?

Answer: You can't see, but you hope all of them.

Question: Why have you never been here before? Cops get a 25% discount on boxes.

Answer: Two more shots.

You shift right and catch sight of the perp's stiffening legs. You're both down on the floor of the donut diner, rolling in the dirt with an unlucky fat guy. You try to meet his eyes through the ski mask but he stares up at the ceiling fan which spins forever.

NADIA BELHADJ

It's not the gunshots. It's the silence that comes after.

Outside Little O's, the sounds of bullets echo and spray as I flee through the parking lot. Each step, the resistance grows, like when you are underwater and for those brief seconds the stuff above the surface ceases to exist. Andre ceases to exist.

My feet hover the few blocks to the car. I tear off the mask and my hair celebrates its freedom. The replica goes into my waistband. I'll toss it in the first river I cross.

Once they know his identity, they'll come for his friends first. I might get a day's head start. What if I left a hair, a fleck of dead skin, or a fiber of clothing? What if I can't leave my boyfriend behind?

Slowly, traffic noise emerges. I've surfaced. The sound which came after the shot is the one I can't unhear. Did I even catch it? A millisecond of impact. The exhalation of the man who would do anything for his family. And my feet tapping the parking lot as I stride away. Andre took the bullet so I'd be free. But I'll never be free of that sound.

I'm nearly at the car now. Not many people on the street. Fumbling the keys, I struggle against the door. When it's open, I drive. The bag of till money rides on the passenger seat where Andre should be.

People who say moments like that go by in a flash are wrong. The sound after the shot collapses into a black hole that sucks everything in. You flee. You get in the car and drive, but how far you go, the gravitational pull of that moment is too strong. It plays with you, lets you extend the tether of distance, watching you on the freeway before hauling you back, gripping your lungs, twisting your head, forcing you to watch the terror in the eyes of the mother covering her stroller, the chairs that scattered when the big guy hit the deck, the spray of red on the linoleum, and the labored breaths.

And then the engine makes a sound. A rattle. Another noise that becomes part of the black hole, smashed back into that moment. Air pummels through the gap in the window, and you're cold. The sweat of the mask was years ago. The money next to you will never pay its debt. It will barely cover a few weeks on the road.

HARRY KATAR

The outrage has grown since the shootout at Little O's a few days back. I've known about the decline of this town for some years. Why would it shock me? Violence abounds.

I knew about the slow death of this place when I signed up for the army. I knew about it when I left. When I came back, it was worse — a dog starving to bones.

When dogs get kicked enough, they'll fight back. Take right now, for instance. My right hand is smashed. I can't reach for my gun, throw a punch, or do anything but curse. This dog fought back.

They got me good — the kid and his grandfather. Me, palms on the table, waiting for the cash, then the kid comes up behind me and slams a claw hammer down. Jackpot on the right hand then a second hit to the left index finger. I hear the bones crack as the metal thuds the wood table.

Green bills flutter to the floor.

I scream and turn my useless hands into fists, but they don't clench.

The kid faces me down. The whites of his eyes are red. Every sinew in his neck bulges to tearing point.

He must be seventeen, eighteen. By the time of conviction, he could get time in the federal pen. He might never get out.

But I can't report this. I can't even go to the hospital. The Caramuccis have their own doctor on call. Basic equipment, but he'll prescribe whatever painkillers I want.

It's a strange feeling not knowing what to do with your hands. That's all I work with most days. Signing papers, taking cash, and giving threats or beatings.

I didn't even get to the part in the playbook where I had to punch up pops a little.

The room is barely big enough for the three of us. Grandpa stands to my left, across the round table. We all back into the peeling walls, the paper looking like something out of the Simpsons.

The kid, tall and wiry, breathes through his teeth. We look at each other and I feel the world through my hands. Maybe that's why painting heals me. I create a new reality with the weapons that usually maim and kill.

What do you do when a punk is staring you down with a hammer, and all you have is arms to swing? Dogs who fight to die don't stand back and bark, they go for the neck.

"Get out," he says, a picture of calm. Then he stands aside. He lowers his hammer hand, but grips it so tight my own palms feel it.

By the time I call this in, they'll be gone. The house will be left to rot with others.

I'm mad at myself really. This will put me out of action for weeks. I take one last look at the scene and make for the door.

The warm air outside stings my hands. They'll balloon if I don't find ice. The car keys slip out of my grasp. Trying to get them in the car door is agony.

I wonder where the kid and old man will go.

Ray Greene

The door shakes. Hammering, not knocking. Why doesn't he use keys? What took so long? Is Andre hurt?

Gramps opens the door and I stand behind him. He tells the police they ain't coming in. That's right.

Why do they always come in pairs? One has fat red arms sprouting from his shirt, the other is too short.

I peer into the squad cars behind, both of them. No Andre.

As the words 'I'm afraid to inform you' come out of the taller one's mouth, the hallway falls under torrents of water. It pins me down and floats me at the same time.

"Andre Greene was killed in an incident at the Little O's store around sixty minutes ago."

I barely hear the words. They're muffled, and the pressure of the water does its best to burst my ears.

Gramps crumples and somehow floats back into the kitchen.

Nadia and Andre look down from their boat. It's full of used bills. The money's getting wet, they say. I have to swim up.

The shorter cop has his hands on my shoulders. "Identify the body." He says it over and over.

I've never been in the back of a cop car before. No cuffs and the grill stays open.

"Am I a suspect?" I ask. Could you think of something stupider to say, Ray? A suspect for what?

"You are eighteen, right?" He says.

"Not until next week."

My skin feels slick. My feet are flippers, unable to walk to the squad car like a human. I flounder into the back seat. My brain forgets everything except the last four seconds. I have to identify my brother. My brother is at the station.

He sighs and tells his partner that Gramps has gotta come too. He makes this awful noise.

The back seat of the car is dark. Black seats and an ugly metal grill. My head brushes the roof. What will they say at school?

My grandfather can't look anywhere but ahead. We don't speak. Our tongues are eels, waiting to lash out, but waiting for the moment. He holds my hand and his grip is dry. Dry and weathered like a rock.

Principal Joyce

When you're the principal, everyone looks to you for decisions. Usually, it's to criticize. Now, it's to see if I remember CPR. I mean, we all did the training.

I slide to my knees on the court floor. Someone is already running to get the defibrillator, calling 911, I'm sure.

Apart from a vaguely furrowed brow, he lies on his back, peacefully. His eyes look up to the rafters like there's a ball stuck up there.

I'm glad I can't see what the students are doing. A deafening silence envelopes the hall, then hushed whispers. They stand up, sit down, jabber advice, claw their arms and legs.

My hands go up and down in compressions so hard I think I'll crack his breastbone. He's still in good shape for his late fifties.

Each compression I feel my arms getting stronger like this is the best exercise my skinny frame could get. It's like I'm trying to bring the whole school back to life and I'm terrified it's too late. It's not too late. Don't you die on me, Primley. You can't imagine the paperwork I'll have to send to the super. If he could, he'd laugh that Woody Woodpecker laugh of his. Instead, he stops breathing.

I don't see them, but the shadows on the high lights tell me there are dozens crowded around, unable to come closer than arm's length for fear of disturbing the reviver. But they inch forward as if an invisible bungee restrains them. Their own hearts pound hard enough to give Primley strength and they rattle like addicts in their helplessness.

I blow three breaths, more compressions, and repeat for two minutes, maybe more.

My dream was the same as Primley's — to walk out of here. But we're both stuck in a tired school gym, lip to lip, palm to chest, principal to coach. No carpentry shop for me. No peaceful afternoons turning wood and applying a coat of lacquer.

The ambulance won't arrive for at least ten minutes. We don't exactly live next to Johns Hopkins.

There are hundreds of shadows around me now. They all look down waiting for an end-of-year decision. How long do I keep going before I stop? When I do, I'll be the one that kills him.

AFTER

Coach Primley

I add a spoonful of sugar to my iced tea. Sit back on the stoop, stir the cup, and watch life go by. And they say sugar kills. The paper boy rides past and flings one onto the deck.

Time used to go in one direction only. Down, down. If you look down, it grips your feet and pulls you further, further, till you get to six feet under. The shot clock always drains to zero.

Now I don't look at the clock. The time is set by the paper hitting the mailbox, my neighbors driving to work, or the basketball sun reaching its peak. The newspaper headline staggers me. *Graduation Tragedy at Woodfield High.*

I look up and Marta's there, waiting at the door in silence.

"What's on for later?" I ask.

She smiles back. Sometimes it's dinner and television, other times we go dancing. I might not be as quick as in my college days, but I can still move my feet.

Some kids are throwing a football and it scuffs the stoop.

I get off my chair and scoop the ball up. Arm drawn, I think back those forty years to when I threw a mean spiral.

The four kids look at me, heads cocked, as I throw the ball high. It goes up, up into the orange evening. It fades in the sky as it travels back in time, past streetball games as a kid, siblings leaving town, early funerals, bad news in the maternity clinic, the highs and lows of each season, and the greatest honor of giving a speech to people who relied on me.

I feel their hands underneath me, lifting me up. Distant voices. A scoreboard appears overhead and the numbers tick up. When I look back at the stoop, Marta has gone inside. The time on the scoreboard marches forward to infinity and the ball gets higher and higher in the sky. I decide to go after it.

KYLE RADLEY

Dear Roger,

How is purgatory? It might surprise you that I'm asking your opinion, but I'm writing this letter because I need some advice.

The next part might not surprise you. I got a girl pregnant. Stereotype, right? High school senior with decent grades and a full ride to college fucks things up. But then, you're an expert on that too.

Her name is Hayley. We go to school together but we're not together. In fact, I'm not sure I'm able to do the whole marriage thing. It was one time, at a party — another cliché, right? Maybe Mom told you I don't go out with girls cause I'm focusing on basketball. Truth is I had to try it once. I can't really express it, but it's not me.

When Mom became pregnant, how did the conversation go? Was it an ultimatum? I don't know why she's still on your side after all those out-of-town trips. If I come to the prison, will you tell me the truth of it all?

Giving up college is not an option, but that means I can't do right by Hayley and I'd leave this child as torn up as I am. Playing is the only thing that makes sense to me — Coach Primley's instructions, the angles of the court, the way your shoulders scream, the fact your teammates would die for you.

I guess what I'm asking is 'can you explain any of this?'

Your son, Kyle.

P.S. Coach Primley passed away from a heart attack. He didn't even get to retire. Funeral is next week.

Roger Radley

I've got twelve words in my head. None of them are worth anything on their own, but together, they unlock five million dollars on a cold storage crypto wallet. Almost every night I go to sleep doing the math on the value of each of those words; when I wake up, the words morph into fists and eyes and sweat-stained prison uniforms.

My cellmate, Malone, has gone through all the options with me. He's survived supermax before and came back for a second visit. The options are as follows:

Give up the keys to the 5 million dollar fortune. Do this and I won't last a week. Only reason I'm not dead, Malone says, is the possible reduced sentence that my passwords offer another inmate.

Promise the money to one of the shot callers. Join his crew and 'survive the five'. Likely, the state will add time for any misdemeanor. My family won't see a penny of the money I worked my life for.

Find an 'outside guy'. The FBI has watched my wife and business partners, tracking every message for years. My only hope was Kyle. *Was*. They can't follow minors. He hasn't said a word to me since his last birthday.

None of those three options work for me. Malone said he's already been offered a cut if I go for option two. He's good at persuading, he said. He's the one who broke my ribs even though I suck his dick each night. I thought clandestine visits to gay bars would make me happy once, but now I know the only thing that will bring me peace is Kyle and his mom getting that money.

The mail trolley rumbles along the D-wing gallery, past cells twelve and thirteen. For the first time since Malone's wife sent him the divorce papers, it stops in front of our cell.

"Radley," announces the guard from the other side of the door.

It takes a good twenty seconds to get down from the top bunk. Each grip of the rail sends shockwaves through my ribs. Malone took my Vicodin too.

The guard screams through the hatch that if I don't take my mail in the next three seconds it goes back on the truck.

It takes a good deal of effort to raise my right arm to the hatch. "Thank you, officer."

I tell Malone it's just more papers from my lawyer, but I recognize the handwriting. *Kyle.*

If this letter contains more than a 'screw you' from my son, option three is back on the table.

CATHERINE SCHWARZ

"Your key, Mrs. Schwarz."

I'm not sure I even thank the receptionist. Maybe I just sigh. How am I going to get up tomorrow? How am I going to put my jacket on the stand in the office and plop down into my chair? How will I nod along with all the latest developments in cases I couldn't give a damn about? Yes, we have a stable income, but lawyers go through it all — grabby bosses and systems which are designed to be openly unfair. Are German sedans and meeting-room croissants supposed to make up for being an also-ran? Will my supermax fraudster still be there next week, or will broken ribs turn into a cracked skull? Yes, a reduced sentence would look better on my record, but I don't blame him. He didn't break the law, and I can prove it.

The room teems with must. No one has been in here for days, not even the cleaners. How will I sleep in dusty sheets? I've always wondered what the charm of motels is. Whisky from the bottle and watching the coin-operated television. Except there's no whisky here.

How will I talk to my mother, knowing she's giving up, ditching the meds, and leaving me to face this alone? It's cancer I hate, not her. And how will I find a new job for Manny?

Suddenly, I'm tired. It's past midnight. I lay down on the bed. The mattress groans even though I'm one hundred fifteen pounds. As I gaze up at the yellowish glow on the ceiling, I feel my whole life on top of me, waiting to crush me in my sleep.

Why was it me who left? It should be Peter grinding his teeth in a local motel. I should bill him for my stay when the divorce goes through. I'm done playing nice. Single mothers can still do a great job. Mine did. Why should I give up on having a baby? Why should I give up my career?

I switch off the lamp and close my eyes. It's hard to know how much sleep I'll get, if any. My mind races through my list of tasks for tomorrow. I'll call my mother. I'll fix what I said. I'll get a better deal for my client — at least get him out of that hellhole prison. I'll get representation before Peter does anything stupid.

But the hardest thing about a to-do list is putting yourself at the top.

Beth Schwarz

One of the nurses the agency sent was wonderful. She told me how it will go down. That's what she called it, 'going down', like it's a drug deal and not an old lady dying. She said the weight falls off you, the pain increases, and the painkillers go up too. At the end, you won't feel it, but that could take months. She said most nurses do their jobs and avoid questions.

I'm sitting here now with Manuel and my cup of tea. We're watching Wheel of Fortune again and for once it's going well. She's on for the jackpot.

"Can you take the chair outside, Manny?" It's nice out, and I'm not sure how many more times I'll sit under the midday light. "The sun is one of the few things that feels alright."

When we're sitting in the front garden I make my little speech. "Manuel," I say, "you've been like a son to me."

He looks at me, terrified of what comes next.

"I'm sorry we haven't gotten you a job, a real job."

He says he's grateful, that he's liked living with me.

Horsecrap, I think. I'll say this for the young man, he's polite and he's well turned out — always wears an ironed shirt, no matter the heat. "I'd like to help you, but you've got to do one thing for me first."

"Yes, Mrs. Schwarz."

I spent the first sixty-something years of my life patching things together, and now here I am ripping bandaids off left and right. It worked a charm with

Catherine. Here goes. "Manny, I want you to help me die."

He looks up and down the street. No one overheard us. We don't do the nosey neighbor thing here.

A car turns onto the street but reverses when the driver realizes it's a dead end.

"How do you mean, Mrs. Schwarz?"

So I tell him. I tell him I'm not on board with transforming from an invalid into a crushed little songbird with no meat on my bones. I tell him I've worn my last diaper. I tell him about a method involving a cocktail of barbiturate drugs all popped into one drink. We can schedule it a few days from now to give me time to say my goodbyes. I tell him there's nothing to come back on him, I just want somebody there to hold my hand, and it can't be my daughter. I tell him to wipe the place of his fingerprints and leave for a couple of days. I tell him it was Catherine's idea but in reality, she doesn't know yet. Not sure if she'd approve. I tell him after it's over, he can stay in the house as long as he likes. He'll get on his feet, take the cash in my secret tin, maybe drive on home if that's what he wants, or start anew.

"There will always be a lady needing a man in a clean shirt," I say.

Inside, the TV erupts with a round of applause and whooping.

I bet he never thought he'd be lost for words around me. Manuel sits there, dumbly, knowing the answer to the final puzzle, but not wanting to say it.

"I'll take that as a yes."

Manuel Hernández

List of reasons to kill Mrs. Schwarz:
- She asked me to. It is my duty.
- She would do the same for me.
- If I say yes, she'll arrange things with Catherine — new job, a place to stay.

List of reasons not to kill Mrs. Schwarz:
- American prison
- I'll always know.
- Things will be weird with her daughter.

I can't believe I actually wrote this list. It's not that long. I mean three against three, like an American baseball game, tied in the ninth inning. The longer I sit in my room, writing things down on pieces of paper, this distance grows. She's only in the living room, but I have to check on her every hour, *más o menos*.

I put one of my Juan Rodrigues tunes, "La Banda Guatemalteca." By the end of it, I have to make my call. When is she thinking of doing it? The longer I leave the decision, the crazier this idea seems. It's hard to explain, this feeling, but it's a different kind of ache to when I left my real mother. If I do this, it's like I'm killing both of them.

The song tells the story of a hero who goes out to war in the ganglands. The phrasing of the lyrics, the little interruptions of brass, and the punch of the rhythm — that can make any story convincing. *You can't be a hero if you don't take the shot.* That's not actually a line in the song but it could be. Sometimes, the heroes are the people stuck at the bottom, not those on top. Maybe that swings it. Maybe being a hero is the fourth item on the list. Maybe.

Eduardo Lopez

It's tomorrow and I haven't left yet. I sit in my car and watch the Moonlight hit Lake Pinner.

After texting those *pendejos* at Rubicon, I went back to the residence. Rent's not due for a few days, but I told my daughter I'm coming home, so it's a one-thousand percent done deal (her words).

My hundred bucks is too tight for celebrations. There's no celluloid moment where I smack golf balls into the lake and howl into the night. No six-pack of brewskies with a buddy. No buddy actually. The guy I was friendly with at the residence moved to Boston and changed his number.

I exit the car and walk along the shore. This place ain't so bad, but it's nothing without family. I can't imagine turning fifty here. When you pay to get across, they don't tell you you'll be lonely.

Not many stars tonight. I spark the last cigarette in the pack and skirt the water's edge by the sound of lapping waves alone. Just like back in Michoacán. A ten-hour day on the *aguacate* grove wrecks your back, and the dust sits in your lungs. One hundred eighty pesos ain't much but it pays for gas and a full cooler.

A couple of kids in the no-lights pickup see my Marlboro cherry through the night air. This high schooler leans out and says "Hey. Hey. Is that weed?"

"You a narc?" I reply. Then a laugh bursts out. "Just a regular old smoke."

He seems disappointed.

"You know anyone who wants to buy a car?" I counter. "Corolla. Good condition. I just want a thousand for it."

He doesn't know how to reply.

Stupid, really. How would they even get in touch? I tossed the cell into the lake ten minutes back. "Never mind, kid," I say. "I'll find someone." One last drag on the cigarette, then I crush it in the dirt.

The cell is gone, and Eduardo Lopez can't be traced. When he goes over the border it won't be through the checkpoint. It won't be with his hospital security badge and sterilized scrubs. It will be midnight. He will spend every darkened hour crawling through the scrubland in some arid dust hole between Arizona border towns. Like returning to the womb. And three days later, he'll arrive in Michoacán, sign the *finca* work register, take a gun from the *autodefensas*, lower his eyes and duck his head under the low front door, suffer the accusations of his family, hand over a few crumpled dollar bills, all the ones that remain after four years *en el norte*, then he'll lift his eleven-year-old daughter up to eye level and say, 'Sweetie, we're going to the lake.'

Ruby Carson

List of chores:

- Wash the sheets at the laundromat. Tell them hot water.
- Sweep the stoop and clear the leaves from the drain pipe.
- Get the groceries in exchange for a few hours of bagging.
- Remember to block the broken part of the door with a chair
- Clear the bottles from the back yard.
- Borrow the vacuum from the Neales next door.
- Ask Joanna for the latest English assignment. Have something to give to Mr. Bush.
- Talk to DeShawn about Uncle Néstor. See if he can help.

List for Momma's next paycheck:

- A phone (even if it's a burner)
- A backpack and shoes for school. No more questions from teachers.
- A new pan with a handle that doesn't burn your hand.
- To get my hair rebraided
- Appointment with the dentist. She won't get a job with broken teeth.
- A real notebook, so I can stop writing lists on torn newspapers, and start writing down all the things I can't say to Kayleigh from CPS.

KAYLEIGH HARRIS

"**W**hat is your name, Madam?"

"Kayleigh Harris."

"Is this the first time you've inquired about adoption?"

I tell her it is, but it's not. A few years back I called another agency. It was right after Mark left and right after I found out it was me not him. Unable to conceive. Kind of ironic, as though God smited me for messing up the first one, some thirteen years back.

We set up the initial appointment and I make a list of some of the things she mentioned. *Assets, plan for work, family support, schools nearby, reasons for, reasons against.* It doesn't take me more than a minute.

Is there any guarantee? No. Will I be able to keep my job and provide the care she needs? Not unless I move back with my own mother. Why does it always come to this?

The coffee pot boils and I pour a cup. Somehow, this break between appointments seems to be going at normal speed. My fingers itch for something to fret about. I sit on the settee and flip through the home-design magazine my mother brought me last week. When I think about it, her idea is not a terrible one. Three generations of girls, living it up on her ranch outside of town.

My phone buzzes. It's probably Henry, scheduling another emergency call out or head office chasing paperwork. Unknown number.

"Hello," I say. The coffee coursing through my bloodstream overrides the weary voice I intended to use.

On the other end of the line, there's a crackling. Breathing.

"Hello? This is Kayleigh Harris. What's the purpose of your call?" I sit a little straighter. Still no reply. My eyes shift to the window as if someone is watching this strangely sad prank call.

And then, a child's broken voice. "Miss Kayleigh?"

"That's right." I try to keep my voice light and playful. "Now, who is this I'm talking to?" I know it's Ruby.

"We met at the hospital last week."

I bury the images of this poor kid with a three-day hunger. Instead, the care checklist moves to the front of my mind's eye. "Are you ok? How can I help you?"

There's another long silence on the line.

I know whatever she says next, I'll have an answer, a next step, someone or something that can make her safe. Then I'll call it in to CPS. This is what I do.

HENRY CAUDRY

Ten things you wish you could say to your daughter, but you're concentrating on breathing:

Does this bullet make us equal? It doesn't hurt, but all the strength I kept inside these years is bleeding out. *It's leaking through my hands, onto the polished floor.*

You know what I do for a living, trying to put broken families back together again. Mostly it doesn't work. Sometimes, you really are too sensitive. But the way we treated you when you came out was wrong.

I have left your mother's church. We nearly broke up because of that. Apart from going six months without speaking to you, that was the hardest thing I've ever done. We've started counseling, and you are the only one who knows.

How can we de-escalate the situation with your girlfriend? We really do want to meet her. *The police are doing a bad job of de-escalating this situation.*

I'd like to understand the job you do, but I'm a dinosaur. Help an old man out and explain all those zeros and ones. *One gunshot. Zero feeling in my legs. One half-eaten donut, zero sips of coffee, two cops, two bullet wounds, and the two of us.*

If I don't make it, promise you will talk to your mother. It will kill her if you don't, and I can't have that on my conscience too.

If I don't make it, don't give me some hero's funeral. *Door's still open. The air is hot, but my legs are cold.*

All I ever did was put your life in front of mine.

I can't think of any more things to say to you.

You'd have something smart to say if you were next to me. Why aren't you here to say it?

MOLLY CAUDRY

When I don't see him milling around with a coffee in the parking lot, I fight through the crowd.

Cops at the door push me back and I say, 'I'm the daughter. I'm *his* daughter. I *need* to see him.'

The door opens, the cop steps aside and fear catches in my throat like my neck hit a tripwire.

I taste the nosebleeds I had as a kid, iron red trickling down my gullet.

Three lumps on the floor. They are immovable stone sculptures.

White-suit photographers swarm the place. Nobody talks.

By the window, there's a red-haired lady cop laid out.

Those millions of boxes collapse into the darkest one.

The guy who pointed at me and fired stares upwards.

Heaven is blocked by faded tiles and a ceiling fan.

They took his mask off at least. He's young.

The air won't go in, won't come out.

Henry lies there. Face up. Belly up.

The murmurs around cut to zero.

My coffee-machine heart grinds.

Loafers make his feet look tiny.

His too-tight wedding band bites.

Only a truck could pull him out.

A white ghost under a beard.

What was he trying to say?

The cop speaks. I kneel.

'He's gone,' they say.

No pain, they say.

'No touching.'

'Yes,' I say.

It's strange being this close but not being able to hold his hand. He looks tired of trying. My mother will blame me of course. She'll blame Janine too. The ceiling feels lower and lower and I'm lying on the linoleum, just to get down to eye level, our heads one foot apart, staring, wishing he could know I came to Little O's on purpose, and that I really wanted to spend his half-hour break together, and that I really wanted that donut. And now, all that's left in my head is the smell of cinnamon sugar and those millions of possible universes swirling in a storm of unwritten code.

Janine Bowen

"You think he wanted to be buried?"

Molly looks at me like I just trod on her dad's chest. "Not here," she whispers. Of course, the churchyard was not his own idea. "Who buys a couple's plot for an anniversary gift?" Her mother. That's who.

We practiced this for days, talking through the route we would walk to honor her father. Stop into the CPS office and get coffee in some other place so the taste of beans and donuts isn't tarnished forever. Smack balls in the batting cage where he and Molly used to go. And then we'd stand outside this palace of bile when all the homophobic turds flush into the dusty-ass graveyard.

When your father dies you change from a princess to a flightless little bird with no wings and no voice and no reaction, apart from a nervous twitch. Even with the makeup and the black dress, Molly is that bird. I grab her by the shoulder and say her father would be proud.

She looks at me with watery eyes, and says, "He was."

My first funeral was my grandpappy's. They played "My Way" by Sinatra and his melodramatic second wife announced right after the song finished that 'He did, indeed, do it *his* way.' People will say anything at a funeral to bring solace to the grieving. Who knows what kind of lies they spread in a church clique? They will have called him a hero, despite the fact the perp and the cop bled out on the floor next to him.

"Get ready. They're coming out."

We stand in the middle of the path under the threatening sky. It's the same color as the felt on the cubicle of the office where I no longer work.

The first mourners, all members of this evil congregation stiffen as they see a queer couple with sexy black dresses, and streaks of pink and blue running through their hair.

I grip Molly's hand, almost crushing it.

They won't be milling around, patting each other on the back. They want to avoid us, and we get ten minutes with the casket after the show. That was the deal.

"Don't focus on them," I say. "They'll be harassing some diner waitress soon enough." About twenty people filter out and turn to the right to go the long way back to their cars. Her mother doesn't even look, she just follows the crowd. It's hard to see her face under the ridiculous hat.

Molly stands there, frozen.

"When we get in there," I say, "tell him he saved you, even if the bullet was missing. Tell him you never looked back, and you won't." If she can't say it, I will. That's the only way to clear the smoke that's forever rising from the gun that shot him.

Enid Stanford

Gilligan pushes his 'super sundae' to the middle of the table. He has grown puffy gills. Would I tolerate this kid if he wasn't my flesh and blood? Look at him, wiping his mouth on his sleeve.

The sundae oozes over itself, the spoon in the middle, erect, like a pole without a flag. He looks at me for instruction.

"Why won't your mother let you eat ice cream?" I ask.

He stares at the table. "I'm just not allowed it."

"You know, when I was in high school, I used to come here Friday nights."

Gilligan looks up at my wrinkled face, the cogs turning in his mind that someone like me could ever have been just a few years older than him.

"It was different back then."

It sure was. Same booths, similar food, certainly, but the conversation now is hushed, and there's no bell to ding the orders.

Gilligan looks at me with Puss in Boots eyes. "You want to try?"

"Go clean yourself up," I say. "We've got a long drive back." I'm not sure exactly why we drove here. Autopilot I suppose. I haven't visited for over ten years. Not since Vincent passed. I look for some kind of keepsake to take. Maybe I shouldn't push my luck.

My grandson goes to the bathroom and I give my daughter both barrels via text. She's lucky it's not all in caps.

No more looking after the boy. I say. *I'm serious.*

I consider whether to call her a bad mother. That's what she called me. More than once.

You earn six figures but your son can't stay out of trouble for six minutes.

When I get the check, I slip the waitress a fifty. Her eyes grow to saucers before she reins it in and tries to play it cool. "Thank you so much, ma'am."

"Don't call me ma'am," I tell her. "I used to cause trouble in here forty years back."

She smiles like she doesn't believe me, but then I give her the stare I usually reserve for Gilligan at his worst or for no-good security guards.

We walk to the car and the roar of traffic hits us. "Forty-five minutes to home," I say.

Gilligan gets in the back like I'm his chauffeur. It's ok, I won't give *him* both barrels. I'll use the silencer for him.

I'll use the drive to decide whether I'll call the tackle 'assault'. Will that change Gilligan's mother back into my daughter? It won't make a bit of difference to him.

The station wagon hits the highway and we drive.

"Can you turn on the radio?" says a voice from the back.

I don't answer.

JOEY BROWN

"Honey, I'm sitting in a diner with a newspaper in my hand."

"... that's what you said after you left the PD," she says.

"Yes," I say with a sigh. I'm suspended from my poor-paying job. I don't tell her the intruder I floored was a grandmother. The only weapon she had was probably the hairspray in her car. I don't tell her I'm safe from misconduct, but they'll find a reason to can me anyway. Any reason.

The Jamaican waitress barely took my order before launching into the story about the Donut joint. "It's all over town," she said nervously. I'd tell her my heart runs blue, but it's numb. I've heard at least three completely different versions of what happened this morning. Looking for the links in all the stories is pointless because nowadays there are too many personal truths.

My wife spins a story about how she's feeling better. Some new opportunity has come up.

"That's great," I say. She gets defensive if I ask questions like 'how much' and 'when'.

A clatter of plates from the kitchen almost makes me drop the phone. Some of the coffee jumps from my cup onto the table. "I'm coming home soon," I say. "Just a couple of calls to make."

A father in the booth next to mine explains to his two-and-two family that shootings only happen in places where God permits it. As if the button-down shirt you wear to church can stop a bullet. I almost say something. In the end, my jaw clamps shut, just like it did in the office. Will I tell my boy or will I come up silent then too? *Nothing's going to change, son.* The lie that every father tells at some point.

The call with Leticia ends and my cup sits on the table. Should I even spend the $1.75 on a piece of pie?

I scroll the feed of job advertisements in the area. It goes on. Thousands of half-lies, those vague job descriptions with missing insurance policies and $12-$17 wage ranges (which really mean $12-$13).

The job advertisements are just procrastination. The call I really have to make is to my brother. I know I still owe him. 'What's another couple of thousand?', I'll say. I'll tell him Leticia's working and that next year, things will be better.

LETICIA BROWN

"We're at the sports store, honey. Can we talk at home later?"

Joey needs to tell me over the phone, he says. Same as after his police dismissal.

Honestly, the day I feel good enough to take a step forward, to apply myself, to get out of the house, he gets suspended. And just after I signed over our car as collateral for a two-thousand dollar loan.

"The sales seminar is next week," I say.

The silence tells me Joey's not enthused.

It's not just Jackson's future hanging between us, there's a kind of dead air on the line. There's something Joey's not saying. He hasn't talked about money once.

"I love you, you know."

He says he knows.

Last night, when we were clearing dishes, he told me if it wasn't for Jackson, he'd have blown this town to hell and hired a U-Haul after the dismissal verdict. We didn't make love after that. I didn't hold him, and he didn't hold me. Neither of us slept. He knows Dr. Leibowitz says change is not good for me.

Jackson comes back from the counter with his new bat. The handle gleams. A bat is happy whether it clocks a home run, or knocks out a debtor's teeth.

"It's great, sweetie."

His arms hang at his side like an awkward teenage orangutan. He barely talks anymore. It must be girls. It's always girls in high school.

"Go wait in the car."

"What?" says Joey on the other end of the line.

The version of my son who hangs on our phone line is now an orangutan wearing a Dodgers uniform.

Joey tells me more about blocking the boss's family from entering. Now he's on suspension.

My muscles tighten with each sentence. He knows he shouldn't worry me when I'm out of the house.

The balloon inside my head fills. Each problem is a new breath of air.

The voice on the announcement system says the store is closing. I look over at the clerk, half expecting him to look sorry and say my card got rejected. Then I remember Jackson paid with Mrs. Caramucci's cash. A migraine pushes the back of my cranium. Each breath of air in the balloon robs air from my lungs.

"Leticia. You OK?" says a tiny voice from the phone in my hand.

It's hard to tell how fast I'm breathing. I put it back to my ear and say "We can't leave this place, Joey." There's more silence now. Apart from the shuffle of feet in the store. Maybe he's climbed to hang out on the telephone line with his son. Two little monkeys watching a mother's nerves fry.

"Who said anything about leaving?"

There's something he's not telling me.

I steady myself on a rack of suit pants. The material feels slippery and cheap. "This town is part of us. Besides, I've got my sales conference next week."

Joey takes a drink of something. "Just finishing up my coffee," he says.

"Cafes aren't what they used to be," I say. "Nowhere is safe."

We both decide to tell each other our monetary secrets back home, in hushed voices, after Jackson has gone to his room, and before another breathless night with panic ballooning in my head.

AMANDA O'ROURKE

There are so many thousands of questions and procedures and statements and jokes and stories and thoughts you wanted to send out into the world. For example, you want to tell your partner that he should have covered the back exit, but secretly you cheer for the girl, the one with the perfect nails hidden under gloves. The one with her hair squashed flat by a ski mask. The one with deep brown eyes.

They all get further away with each fluid ounce of blood that leaves the hole in your neck. At least your face won't have to be rebuilt in the mortuary.

The closer your partner gets, the harder it is to say his name. To remember even. Radleigh? Rhodes?

Ignore him. Close your eyes in bliss. Feel his heart pound harder than the time you got drunk and had sex at his place. You never talked about it. Each breath of each word hits harder than the bullet. The floor is liquid-soft and you sink. His mattress was a rock and the sheets crusted. Still, he shot the bastard who put that hole in your neck. The pool around you swirls in black and white squares, streaks of red and blue, and crystals of powdered sugar sparkle. A tiny casing lies right in your eyeline.

On another day, you walk into Little O's again and you get more than a 25% discount. In fact, the coffee is free. The music is back, and no dumb members of the dumb public clog the joint. It's full of district uniforms. A couple of sergeants mill around, waiting for their order.

All you manage to gurgle is 'O'Malley's'. He knows —
the partner whose name you can't remember, despite the
fact you've ridden in the same car for months, ever since
the academy. He knows that's the name of the cop bar
where they'll hang your picture, toast you with whiskey
and say 'what a shame.'

You are not ashamed.

Nadia Belhadj

They won't stop. Even without the right evidence. That's what happens when a cop dies. The report barely mentioned who pulled the trigger. It mostly mentioned the 'dangerous gunman' still at large.

I'm sitting in the Camry a few miles from the Canadian border. My clothes are hopeless against the wind. I'd wear the ski mask if I hadn't thrown it. Get away from the crossing, just a few hours' trek, then back onto the road and pick up a ride to Winnipeg.

I'll need to make up some story about my surprise visit to my aunt, but we look similar enough that I can use her passport to fly to Marrakech. My breath steams against the windshield. No time like the present to better my Arabic, roll back years of American culture, and settle into an abusive marriage.

My hands have formed into claws that will forever grip the wheel. Every mile I drove, Little O's diner drove with me. Two days without talking to anyone but a few words to the gas station clerks. "Thanks. Just this."

The town I left behind won't escape from Little O's either. All this cause and effect weaves together. Sounds like something Andre's dumb little brother would spout over a trap beat.

My mind casts forward to my pumps crunching the gravel in the parking lot. One look back at the Camry that got me here in one piece, then over the fields at dusk. Hike till morning. The cash in the bag now has cookies and milk for company. The company I thought I'd have for the rest of my life is lying face-up in a police morgue.

As I walk, the sounds of that morning will dampen. I start to hear the calls of birds, the wind rustling trees. My feet tell me where to go, and the hands that gripped the wheel hurt. The air carries the Manitoba winter. My senses return, one by one, and I start again. Dre's family won't be so lucky. I won't be able to send them any cash even when I'm safely in Morocco.

I open the Camry door and look at the hills in the distance. The steam that was trapped in the car with me evaporates in the air.

HARRY KATAR

They watch me, the 'artists' on my side of the circle. Today's model it's a stack of geometric bricks. Perspective, size, shadow. All the bricks are the same type of gray. All the artists too, except me and the goth chick who sits with her back to the wall like an untrusting cat.

I grip the paintbrush in the second and third fingers of my left hand. My crooked index finger points at the canvas, unable to tighten around the brush. The bandages on the other hand stays on for two more weeks.

"It's mostly my pride that's hurt," I say to no one in particular.

The teacher says it's good to have me back. He touches my forearm, just above the bandages. He's about the same age as me — between new father and mid-life crisis. But he ain't military. Maybe he's just into me.

There's no sketching in pencil for me. I use a thin brush.

Piped classical music tries to add some grace to the classroom. The chairs are less comfortable than when I went to school. No coffee and wafers. But, after two weeks without pay, I'm damned well going to use the classes I bought.

A silver-haired lady with a wild-turkey neck turns and tuts out of sympathy. We've only just started the thirty-minute draw and she's spent most of the time trying to catch my eye to give me sympathy. I can't take it. If you accept pity, you grant it to others. That doesn't fit with my line of work.

I can barely hold the brush straight with my splinted finger. Each stroke sends shock waves up my forearms. The bones are still weak. They'll ache on winter days.

"Art is supposed to be torture," I say, deadpan, when the old lady turns again.

In reality, it's torture I can take, as long as I create a new reality. One that's different from the desert valleys of Afghanistan. Maybe that kid and grandfather find a better reality too.

Lifting the brush from the painting, I assess my work — ten lines, some light-gray shading, and a whole lot of empty canvas.

Ray Greene

Items to take before the Caramucci's return:
- Grandpop's last prescription
- Andre's jewelry (until it's sold piece by piece)
- Nadia's iPad — locator switched off
- Dad's state ring — no JUCO games for me
- Andre's truck — pray for a full tank of gas
- Mom's ashes — we'll take that trip to the coast after all
- One thin mattress — take it in turns to sleep
- Gloves and a hat for the old man
- Andre's license — might pass to get a server's job
- Cell phone — location switched off

List of items to leave behind:
- The PS5 Andre was going to buy me
- IHOP door pass and uniform
- High school diploma
- The only house I ever knew
- The team
- Coach Primley
- Andre's body, lying in the basement of the police station, waiting for a funeral
- The town that made it all happen.

Principal Joyce

A Letter to the Woodfields School Community

It is with great sadness that we announce the passing of Randall Primley, loyal servant to our community and beloved coach. Details of his memorial service will be forthcoming. At this time, we ask for no donations, flowers, or messages of support, only that you consider the words below, taken from the speech he was due to deliver to the graduating students before his unfortunate passing.

Whatever you do has consequences. Do something smart, and you'll reap the rewards. Come from the wrong part of town, and your whole life will be a struggle. The root of a beautiful action comes from tiny differences in circumstances and tiny deviations in effort. Did you know, if you improve 1% per day for a year, you increase your ability by 37 times? Imagine being 37 times the person you are now. And if you slip, if you go down one percent, you'll lose a tiny fraction of what you already gained. What I'm saying is, it is all worth it — every slip, every painful moment, every relationship, every minute spent reading a book, every missed shot, every tear, every grade, every kiss, every time you look up and see the sun, every funeral, every promotion, every smile, every time you fall to the floor, every squeak of every shoe on this court, every game won and every game lost. It all counts. Everything in our little town is linked by cause and consequence. It's something you'll never escape, even when you leave. But you don't need to escape. Just move forward one percent at a time, and live the best that you can.

Our school, our community, our town, and our lives continue to intertwine and develop, just as Coach Primley said. We will always remember him, standing on the court he dedicated thirty years of his life to, waiting to give this speech. We will do our part. We will live the best that we can.

In memory of Randall Primley. 1963-2024

About the Author

Philip Charter is an author and writing coach from the UK. His previous works include two collections of short fiction and *Fifteen Brief Moments in Time*, a novella-in-flash. He lives in the Canary Islands, Spain.

112 Harvard Ave #65
Claremont, CA 91711 USA

pelekinesis@gmail.com
www.pelekinesis.com

Pelekinesis titles are available through Small Press Distribution,
Ingram, Gardners, and directly from the publisher's website.

www.ingramcontent.com/pod-product-compliance
Ingram Content Group UK Ltd.
Pitfield, Milton Keynes, MK11 3LW, UK
UKHW041423030225
4424UKWH00017B/95